WHEN *the* NIGHT

WHEN *the* NIGHT

Cristina Comencini

Translated from the Italian by Marina Harss

OTHER PRESS   NEW YORK

Translation copyright © 2012 Marina Harss

Production Editor: Yvonne E. Cárdenas
Text Designer: Cassandra J. Pappas

This book was set in 11.3 pt Janson MT by Alpha Design & Composition
of Pittsfield, NH.

10 9 8 7 6 5 4 3 2 1

Library of Congress Cataloging-in-Publication Data

Comencini, Cristina.
  [Quando la notte. English]
  When the night / by Cristina Comencini ; translated by Marina Harss.
    p. cm.
  ISBN 978-1-59051-511-2 (trade pbk.) — ISBN 978-1-59051-512-9 (ebook)
1. Mothers and sons—Fiction. 2. Landlords—Fiction. 3. Dolomite
Alps (Italy)—Fiction. I. Harss, Marina. II. Title.
  PQ4863.O423Q3613 2012
  853'.914—dc23

                                                          2011047123

And the rib that the Lord God had taken from the man he made into a woman and brought her to the man. Then the man said, "This at last is bone of my bones and flesh of my flesh; she shall be called Woman, because she was taken out of Man." Therefore a man shall leave his father and his mother and hold fast to his wife, and they shall become one flesh. And the man and his wife were both naked and were not ashamed.

—Genesis 2:22–25

There's the not-so that reveals the so—that's fiction.

—Philip Roth, *Exit Ghost*

Night

1

THE STEAK IS in the pan; perhaps I should open a window. The clouds hang low over the Dent du Géant. It's raining up at the alpine lodge, but tomorrow the weather should be fine. I'll take the Germans up to the camp near the summit; let's hope they're as experienced as they claim. They only have to make it past the first slope and over the ledge; after that the final pass is easy. I'll know right away if they're up to it, and then I can always lead them back toward the canyon; they can take pictures of the goats and we'll stop in the woods for lunch.

The light is still on upstairs. She'll switch it off soon; she goes to bed earlier than I do. The baby starts to cry early in the morning. It doesn't bother me, I'm already up. She pushes the baby carriage up and down the meadow at the foot of the hill. She talks to the boy, recounting everything they do, as if he can't see it for himself.

"We'll go visit the cows, and then we'll stop at the bakery for some *krapfen*, how does that sound?"

The child says nothing. I've never heard him speak. One night I heard him crying, for a long time.

Luna didn't talk to our children that way. She let them play in the meadow without supervision. And she was right, even if Clara broke her arm once when she was riding her bike and had to wear a cast for three months. If you don't fall when you're little, you'll fall and kill yourself later, up on the mountain for example.

Damn it! I burned the steak! I'll eat it anyway; I'm not very hungry; in any case, it tastes better when it's burned. Tonight, steak and potatoes. They've been in the refrigerator for a while and I'd better eat them before I have to throw them out. Luna never left the pan on the fire long enough.

"It makes too much smoke."

So what? You can open the window.

"It's cold out."

Tomorrow I'll throw away her clogs. I'm going to get rid of everything she left behind. Little jars, big jars.

"What do you need all that stuff for? Soap is better."

She bought creams and hid them in the refrigerator. And for the kids: markers, pencil cases, toys, clothes.

You only need one pair of shoes per season. That's all. We don't want to be like the tourists who come here in summer to hike and in winter to ski. I guide them up the mountain and all they want is to go up to the lodge and eat. They buy shoes and jackets and it's hot as hell and every year more ice melts.

At first Luna agreed with me. The kids went out in shirtsleeves.

Each of them owned a single sweater. We used laundry soap for everything, even to wash our hair.

Tomorrow I'll throw everything away. I didn't want to get married; she was the one who insisted. I hesitated at first. She was a city girl, but she was strong. She knew how to walk and she had studied. She didn't talk when we went out on the mountain. So I gave in. But I was honest: I told her what I was like, that I know nothing about women, and that my mother abandoned us when we were little. Ran off with an American. I never saw her again. I know she remarried and had more kids in America, because our father told us.

WE WERE DRIVING down to school in the snowcat. Outside, the snow and sky were indistinguishable. When it rains or snows you can't even see the trees. Albert crashed into a tree on his bobsled once. I watched him as he came hurtling down, like a maniac.

He'll get hurt one of these days, I thought.

Our mother didn't allow it; she would yell from the window to slow down because he was frightening her. Then she left, and no one was there to be scared, so he crashed into the trees.

My father was driving in silence, as usual. Suddenly he said: "Your mother remarried and has new children. If anyone bothers you or makes fun of you in the village, you just tell them, My mother is the Snow Queen."

"Who's that?"

Stefan was little and asked a lot of questions. My father was a patient man. I never saw him angry, except that one time. I don't know whether I dreamed it or it really happened. He said to Stefan: "The Snow Queen lives in a crevasse. If she finds a man there alone, she thaws, conceives a child with him, and then goes back to her home in the ice."

LUNA WAS MY Snow Queen, but now she's gone, just like my mother. Except that Luna took the kids with her.

It's easier here without them. I talk to the tourists when I take them up the mountain. They want to hear tragic stories about mountain-climbing accidents, and where to get the best meal. At home I can sit quietly; no one asks me questions, and I don't have to listen to Luna telling me all the town gossip. No kids' noise. They are coming to visit at the end of the month. I'll put away the suitcases she has prepared for them, and pull out their old shoes, T-shirts, trousers. That's all they'll need while they're here. Clara does as I say, but Simon is lazy and hates to walk. But he won't have a choice.

TOWARD THE END, Luna was always buying things: pans, plates, tablecloths. But no one ever came over.

In the early years she was even tougher than I was: only organic food in the house, no one to help her with the house-work, plus a teaching job in the city. On her way to work she would drop off the kids at the nursery, then in the after-noon she would come back and clean, cook, go to bed early, make love. Often and well. She was satisfied, and she fell asleep quickly, her muscular legs gripping mine. Sometimes at night I would switch on the light and stare at her large breasts. I couldn't look at them when we were making love because I was afraid it would make me come; if I touched them I couldn't control myself. Two perfect round mounds, with pink tips. Our children reached for them with their eyes closed, attached themselves to them, trembling, pulled at them, and fell asleep, pink-cheeked, after sucking them dry. Once it occurred to me to pull one of the babies away from her breast and watch him cry.

One night she said to me, "You never touch my breasts when we make love."

"Does it bother you?"

"I didn't say that. I just noticed that you never do."

"Is it a problem?"

"I can't talk to you, Manfred."

"Certain things are not meant to be discussed; you just do them."

Late at night, I graze the tip of her breast with my finger. Her days are long, so she sleeps soundly.

THE STEAK HAS an unpleasant taste. It's overdone. I need to find a woman to screw. Maybe the woman who works at the wood shop; she's not married. She's ugly but she has big tits and she's willing. Karl told me they did it once at the sawmill, with the electric saw switched on to drown out the noise. I won't bring her to my place; I don't want any women in here.

Anyway, I wanted kids. Things went the way they were meant to; it's like the story our father told us in the snowcat. I never saw him look upset because he missed his wife. Except that one time.

He was a man of steel. He raised us by himself, and gave each of us something: the house in the village for me, the lodge to Albert, and the ski-rental business to Stefan. And now he lives in the city. Who would have thought it was possible? After thirty years of managing the lodge with three kids, now he has a dishwasher and thinks that progress isn't such a bad thing after all. Stefan says he has a woman, and perhaps that's why he's so happy to live in town, but none of us knows who she is. I went to see him last Sunday.

WE'VE BEEN SITTING in silence for the last ten minutes. I'm holding a beer. His hands, swollen and tough from years of working in the cold, lie on the kitchen table like two empty shells. Mine will look the same one day.

He asks me, "How are you doing?"

"Fine, and you?"

"Fine. Do you miss your wife?"

"No. You never missed yours."

"I had you."

"Simon and Clara are coming at the end of the month."

"Women don't know how to raise children."

"And yet they're the ones who usually do it."

"Men think it's women's work, but they're wrong. I raised you by myself so I know what I'm talking about. Women don't love their children."

"Everyone says the opposite."

"Because they don't know. How about Albert? How is he doing up at the lodge with his wife? Is she still there?"

"Yes, Bianca likes it there."

"We'll see."

BIANCA IS STRONG, but my father is right. Who knows how long she'll last? Albert says she's happy. Don't be too sure, though; I know something about the happiness of women. It's not their happiness that matters, but their mood. If they're overexcited, that's a bad sign, or if they buy things they don't need, or have trouble sleeping, or stare out of the window in silence. Or if they are too particular and want to argue about everything.

The first few years we were married, I wasn't worried. She didn't ask me why I didn't touch her breasts when we made love. At night I screwed her steadily and calmly; I can go for a long time. Her eyes went from brown to green, and then she looked like a little girl. A little girl and a woman. Then I came.

The last few years, though, she was either too happy or suddenly sad, and when she woke up she had the habit of staring out of the window in silence. She wanted to talk about everything, and no explanation was ever enough. I gave her wine in the evenings, but still it wasn't the same. The green-eyed girl was gone, and the woman I married no longer interested me. But I would never have left her alone with the children. She knew that, so she left me.

Tomorrow I'll give the rest of the potatoes to Bernardo so he can feed them to the pigs. They're disgusting.

I DIDN'T WANT to rent the apartment to that woman. But the real estate agent told me there was no one else in July. Luna decorated the apartment when the carpenter who used to live there died.

"That way we can rent it out to vacationers and make some extra money."

"If we rent it to someone in town we'll have fewer hassles."

"I want to decorate it."

"That way you can buy all the stuff we have no space for."

"What do you care? It makes me happy."

We rented the apartment and made more money, and it changed nothing. Now, I never go inside. The agency has it cleaned, finds the tenants, and deposits the money in my account. This is the first time they've rented it to a woman on her own, but it's none of my business. She's up there, and I'm down here, and it's only for a month.

I have no need for the dishwasher and I never use it. I go to bed early. Tomorrow I'll take two tourists up to the lodge and spend some time with Albert and Bianca. Tonight I'll sleep on the left side of the bed; if you switch sides you don't feel lonely.

2

I PEER OUT OF the window: black mountains, starless sky, silence; leaves rustling, bird calls in the distance. We're in the last house in town. It could be the Middle Ages if it weren't for the landlord's car parked downstairs. I let the corner of the curtain drop back down.

If the baby sleeps five or six hours I'll be all right. Tomorrow I'll take him out early in the morning; we'll go to the meadow to watch the cows graze. He likes them, but they also scare him a little bit. It's cold when we go out. The jagged peaks hide the sun, leaving the valley in the dark. He plays with his toy cars in the grass, *vroom vroom*. When he's not moving around, I gaze up at the pink mountain tops and wait for the sun to warm the air. It's seven in the morning and we're already outdoors.

Tomorrow I'll dress him in his new red woolen jacket and cap, which I bought at the local market. He mustn't catch cold, or else he won't sleep. If he gets a fever, I won't be able to handle it on my own, so far from everyone, without Mario or my mother or anyone else to help me. For now, he's breathing all right; his nose is not too stuffy. If he could just sleep five or six hours straight, or even four, things would be much better. I brought the baby monitor but I don't really need it; the apartment is so small and so quiet that I can hear it when he turns over in bed.

I have to move quietly in the kitchen so as not to wake him. But I'm not hungry, just tired, with an ancient fatigue I've been carrying inside me ever since they put him in my arms at the hospital, wrinkled like an old man and covered in my blood.

AS SOON AS he came out of me, I looked at him and thought, I can't do it.

The nurse scolded me. "Don't squeeze him so hard. Do you want to suffocate him?"

How could she think that a mother would suffocate her newborn child? She was the first to scold me, followed by the pediatrician, my mother, and Mario. In the days after the birth I wanted my mother, but when I saw her arrive I felt like crying, like a little girl.

"Why are you crying? Aren't you happy?"

Everyone kept talking about happiness. Perhaps I had a rock instead of a heart.

I'll never be able to manage, I can't do it.

I didn't tell my mother how I felt, even though I trusted her. Until the problem with the milk began.

I didn't have milk; it just wouldn't come. I'm not a cow. Maybe that's why the baby likes cows so much; he's attracted to their swollen udders. Mine were swollen too, and hard as rocks, but only a few measly drops came out. A joke, a tease. At the hospital, the woman in the bed next to mine woke up every morning with her nightgown dripping with milk.

"I have so much! How will I keep from leaking when I go out?"

The nurse would glance over at me. "Milk is a blessing."

In the morning they brought the babies to us on a cart. I could hear the wheels squeaking down the hall.

I hope he'll suck this morning! So hard that the milk will gush out of my useless breasts like a fountain.

My breasts ached, as if there were stones hidden inside. The nurse would put the baby in my arms; she never let me look at him. She would pick him up brusquely and say, "He has to wake up, he has to eat."

Open your eyes, so she'll stop tormenting you!

The nurse would take my nipple in her hands and move it like a weather vane in front of his tightly shut lips. He would make a face. He didn't want the breast; he didn't like the taste. She would put it in his mouth anyway. The nipple was not part of me, it was something completely separate.

Come on, latch on, that way she'll leave us alone.

I wanted to fall asleep forever next to him.

Don't eat if you don't want to, go back inside, back into the silence and tranquillity, and take me with you.

He would suck weakly from the deformed nipple, with a look of disgust. Then we were alone again, just me and the woman with all the milk. She would talk on the phone with her mother, telling her how much the baby had grown, how much he weighed. Her baby sucked insistently. Mine didn't, and fell asleep quickly. Everything was natural for her: breast-feeding, sleeping, eating. Like an animal. My mother would have put it differently. "It's her maternal instinct. Every woman has it."

What about me? I watched the woman's every movement, the way she shifted the baby from one breast to the other, the way she dried her nipples and attached her bra, how she held him over her shoulder to burp him, how she talked to him.

"That's enough, you'll eat too much and then you'll cry because you have a tummy ache."

It all looked so easy. What was wrong with me? My baby would release the nipple and let it sit there, forgotten, like a cork, a strange beast next to his cheek as he slept. Her baby had black hair, mine was bald. My mother approved. "A newborn should be bald. You were the same."

So it's nothing special.

The milk will come, you just have to believe. It seems you have to believe in milk, and maybe I just didn't believe strongly enough, and that's why it didn't come. My mother tried to reassure me. "It will come, don't worry. I didn't have milk, but you will be more fortunate."

Before falling asleep I would say a prayer: tomorrow, please let me wake up covered in milk, with my nightgown stuck to my breasts like my neighbor. Gallons and gallons of sugary serum; I'll taste it with the tip of my finger. Let it come tomorrow, enough to cover them all, to make my mother envious, to drown that bitchy nurse who looks at me with distaste. I want to see milk everywhere, the bed sopping wet, the baby's mouth full, his weight off the chart, and his diaper full of marvelous yellow shit. All new mothers sniff their baby's shit with a satisfied air, and my mother would like to as well, but my baby barely shits because I don't have enough milk for him.

The nurse said to my mother, "Don't worry, we'll give him formula."

My mother said, "We'll take him home and manage our own way."

She meant *her* own way.

"You have to be relaxed, otherwise the milk won't come."

I had to believe in it, and relax. Instead, I never slept, not even for an hour.

"Take advantage while you're here, because once you get home . . ."

What would happen at home? I thought about this and couldn't sleep. I'll never manage, I thought.

At night I would get up and go to the nursery to look at my baby. My stitches hurt but I needed to be alone with him. He slept soundly while the other babies screamed, ate, cried, lived. He didn't get much milk and so he slept. I was afraid he would go back to where he came from, because of me. That's why I got up at night, to make sure he was still there.

"Don't sleep, stay awake."

The night nurse was kinder than the other one.

"He's small. It will take a little time for him to catch up."

Neither of us had caught up. He looked like a tired old man. All I could see of his nose were two little holes. He had Mario's hands. As soon as he was born, everyone began to take credit for little parts of him: his hands, his feet, his eyes, his nose, his forehead. I put my finger into his little fist; I opened his hand and we stayed like that for a long while. He slept, and I watched him.

Back home, my mother brought a crib and tried to be help-ful. The first few days, my sisters came too. They told me that I had to keep trying to breast-feed, that the same thing had hap-pened to them, but that eventually everything worked out. My mother forced me to eat and gave me beer; she would change the baby and then hand him to me to breast-feed. She and Mario stood there and watched. I looked at the scale for the verdict after each feeding. Just a few grams more; the needle barely moved. Some days I celebrated: he gained twenty grams. I was as happy as on the day I graduated and the examination committee praised my work. Then another setback: he wasn't growing enough.

Mario prepared the formula in the kitchen. He took a few days off work. He wanted to help me, like my mother. I could hear them whisper, so I left the baby in the crib and crept closer.

"Better prepare a bottle. She doesn't have any milk, like me. I knew it right off the bat, as soon as I saw the shape of her breasts. I didn't tell her because I didn't want her to be disap-pointed. But then I thought—well, she's a brunette, and bru-nettes have more milk. That was my hope. But there's no use insisting."

My elder sister has fair hair, but she had milk, so much that she kept it in the fridge and took it to the hospital to feed the premature babies. How can you explain that, *Mamma*, since you know everything?

I wanted to go into the kitchen and tell them: "Take the baby and give him the bottle. Tomorrow I'll start taking the pills to make the milk go away, the milk that never came. That way my breasts will return to their normal size."

I could hear Mario's voice. "Let her try a little longer. It's important, don't you think? For her to bond with the baby."

What bond? To me the baby was still inside of me. We were both in a far-off place, unreachable. They didn't know anything.

Mario spoke to me calmly; he was afraid of postpartum depression. They gave me anesthesia, and I didn't feel any pain. My aunt said that childbirth doesn't count that way; she suffered for twenty-five hours straight and then they had to extract the baby with forceps. *That's* labor. I listened to them and came to the conclusion that since I had not gone through a real labor, it must not be postpartum depression that made me cry every day.

I'll never be able to manage, I thought over and over. The certainty of this made me cry. I couldn't tell my mother or Mario. They were too invested in me. It would have been particularly hard on Mario. My mother had my sisters to worry about, luckily; they all had children with no difficulty at all. It was like drinking water to them.

Mario had only one brother, married to a woman who could do anything. It was important to him that I do things right; for a man, it's like knowing he picked the right woman.

I tried to talk to one of my sisters, who's only one year older than me.

"I'll never manage."

"Don't be silly. It's simple with newborns. They sleep, then you feed them, change them, and take them out for a stroll. Just wait till he's two and can't hold still for a minute!"

I HAVEN'T SLEPT in two years, since he was born and I worried he would never wake up. Now he sits up in his crib at four in the morning and never stops moving. My sister was right.

Mountain villages are depressing at night; the windows are small, there's no light, and no one is out. But the apartment is comfortable and well furnished. In a few days there will be a town fair, maybe I can wear a dress and take the baby down to the piazza. He'll run around and touch everything, but at least we'll have some company for once.

Mario will come at the end of the month and we'll go to the beach, on the island where I've been going since I was a child. What is a month? Thirty days, thirty nights. I'll survive. I didn't breast-feed, but I've taken good care of him for two years. He's a beautiful boy, everyone says so, just a little bit on the thin side and high-strung.

THE PEDIATRICIAN INTIMIDATES me. He's a good doctor—my sisters chose him after much consideration—and he will be good for me as well. He advocates for the child, defends his interests. He doesn't trust me; I'm neurotic, and I don't do the best for his patient. My heart beats hard every time we go for a checkup. I can't answer all his questions, and the baby cries and doesn't want to be touched. As usual, he hasn't grown enough. The doctor asks me if I'm calm, what I feed him, and how often I take him outside. I'd like to punch him, knock off his glasses, and bite his hand, but I answer sweetly, "He's a bit anxious in the evenings, and he has trouble sleeping. He wakes up often during the night and then at six in the morning."

The doctor speaks without looking at me. I'm the last person on earth, a lost cause. "It's all connected to the bond with the mother during pregnancy and the first few months, during breast-feeding."

That word "bond" again. Don't they have another word?

I can no longer think about myself without him. I want to protect him from the world, but sometimes I'm ashamed of both of us. He barely speaks. He says *Mamma*, *Papà*, and he has trouble pronouncing words. Only I can understand him, that's why I can't leave him with anyone. And when he starts to cry, there's no stopping him. Mario is afraid of his crying, especially when he's driving.

I try to control my mind. I can't let myself focus on his crying; it's like music played out of key, boring into your brain. Sometimes it stops suddenly, but don't be fooled: he's just drawing breath so he can cry some more. I talk to him.

"Don't cry, my darling. Come on, don't cry. Stop crying. Why are you crying? Everything is all right."

He climbs up on me and yells into my ear, squeezing my neck. My heart beats wildly. He takes a breath and continues. What is the cause of this terrible sadness? What have I done wrong?

"Stop that, stop that. Everybody's watching, can't you see?"

I'd like to cover his mouth, but then he would cry even more. I have to focus and not let myself be drawn in by his wails. I have to think about something else, squeeze my fists, caress him, console him, until he stops. Silence. I put him down, I breathe, it's over.

NOW I KNOW what to do. I just have to avoid making him cry, be organized, plan ahead, distract him, cook his food and talk to him, play with him, read to him, tell him stories and be patient. Mario sounds calm on the phone. He knows I've learned how to manage, and that I no longer fall apart as I did at the beginning. In October I'll start working half-time, and the baby will go to day care.

I'd like to sleep for ten hours straight, as I used to on the island.

In our bunk beds, my sisters and I would tell each other about our evenings. Parties, boys, dances. I was the best dancer and I fell in love the most. We laughed, and the sound of the sea floated in through the window. The same sea that brought in the shells we kept in a glass bottle. If you opened it, you could smell the stench of death. The crabs in their spiral shells, too scared to come out, were trapped inside.

My sisters are there now, with my mother and their children. My baby doesn't like the sea, it makes him anxious. Why is he so different? The doctor said, "Take him to the mountains for a month."

I have to go to bed, otherwise tomorrow at dawn it will be terrible. I'll open the window just a crack, so we don't end up like those crabs. It's so quiet here in the valley, and the lights are already out in all the other houses. But the light downstairs is still on. The landlord lives there. He's a mountain guide; I wonder how old he is? Forty, maybe younger, but his face is already covered in deep wrinkles. He lives alone but there are two kids' bikes in the entryway. He goes out early in the morning. He speaks with a German accent, like everyone in the town.

"Good morning."

"Good morning."

He spits out the words, without even a glance at the boy, and shuts the door with a bang. From the window, I can see him return in the evening.

This evening I could smell steak and potatoes being cooked downstairs. His light is on. I wonder what he does at night? I don't hear a television, or any other sound. I should ask the girl at the bakery in town.

Good night, mountains, my hour of freedom has ended.

3

MANFRED'S FATHER GUSTAV used to run the lodge up at the mountain pass. Now Albert, the eldest, runs the lodge. They're all crazy."

"Shhhh, speak softly, or else the baby will wake up and I'll have to go."

The girl at the bakery peers at the stroller.

"Can he breathe with that sheet over his face?"

"He can't sleep with the light in his eyes. Why do you say they're crazy?"

The girl wipes the gleaming counter energetically.

"The three boys grew up at the lodge without their mother. In the winter, they drove down to school in a snowcat. Their father would drop them off at the base of the gondola and in the evening he came back to pick them up. He never wanted to settle down with another woman and he never remarried."

"Did his wife die?"

"She ran off to America with a tourist who came to do some mountain climbing. The American stayed for a week; at night he used to play cards with Gustav."

"Goodness . . ."

"No one knows what happened. There are lots of stories. Some people think that the American was rich, but my mother says that the lodge was a good business and his wife never wanted for anything. He gave property to each of his sons. Other people say that she was going crazy up there with him and took advantage of the first opportunity to get out. And some people say that Gustav caught them together and they were forced to run away. Everyone has a theory, but no one really knows."

"She left her three children behind?"

"Yes. She never saw them again, and in America she started a new family."

I move the sheet a little bit, so he can breathe more easily.

"What was she like?"

"I can't remember. My mother says she was beautiful, tall, with dark hair. She did everything. Gustav hid all the pictures of her. There were pictures on the walls at the lodge, with her three boys. Everyone was shocked that she left them behind. Manfred wasn't even ten years old. They all went to school together. He was a sweet boy. He didn't say much, like now. I felt sorry for him. The three brothers were always together; they never made friends, and after school they went back up to the lodge."

"He never married?"

"Who, Manfred? The funny thing is, the same happened to him!"

"His wife left him for someone else?"

"No one knows, but she left. She took the kids with her. People say the Sane boys drive away their wives. Bianca is the only one who's still here. Stefan, the brother who runs the ski rental shop, isn't married, but he has broken up with so many women that no one in the area will go out with him, even though he's handsome and good in bed." She laughs and asks, "Do you want a *krapfen* for your little boy?"

"Yes, thank you. If you wrap it up for me I can give it to him for his afternoon snack."

She takes it from the case and goes on: "Luna, Manfred's wife, left out of the blue. Something happened between them, and she ended up at the hospital. The police questioned Manfred."

"He hit her?"

"Who knows? Manfred is crazy. He would only buy one pair of shoes for the kids—one for the winter and one for the summer. No television, and everyone in bed by nine. Who can live like that?"

"He's a loner."

"A loner? Once he came in here and I asked him, 'How are you, Manfred?' And he answered, 'I'm in heaven. No wife, no kids.' That's what those Sane boys are like."

I pay for the *krapfen*. Best to leave before he wakes up.

"Could you please hold the door so I can get through with the stroller?"

ANOTHER HALF HOUR of walking, trying hard not to jolt the stroller, and then he'll eat without fussing.

What a strange story! The tall, dark-haired mother had probably been unhappy with her husband for a long time. Maybe she was afraid of him or she didn't like him anymore, but she didn't have the courage to leave him. She faked it for years; children fill your days, and then they grow up. What do you do when you don't get along with your husband anymore?

This hill is tiring, and so long! Here we are, we made it. The landlord's car isn't there. I'll leave the boy in his stroller in the entryway so he can sleep. No one ever comes up here anyway. That way I'll have time to cook his lunch. I can see from the window if he wakes up, and after all, he's strapped in. I can always run down and get him. I'll cover his face, so the light doesn't bother him.

I've already cooked the vegetable broth, with a little pasta and chicken. He doesn't like it, he spits it up, but the pediatrician insists that it's good for him.

"He has to get used to eating everything, and to chewing. No more mush, he's too old for that."

I'd like to see him feed my baby.

I open the curtain and look out. The sheet over the stroller is perfectly still. If he sleeps long enough for me to prepare the pasta, then I can change him and I don't have to do two or three things at once, and he won't cry because I'm not holding him. While the broth warms up I'll pee; I can never go when he's around. Just one more peek out of the window.

Still sleeping. He'll be in a good mood when it's time to eat.

What a beautiful day! People in town say that it will rain again in a few days. Let's hope not. What will we do if it rains? We'll be stuck inside.

Think of that poor woman up at the lodge! The winters must have been especially hard. All alone, with three small children. Why do women put themselves in these situations? Then the American came. Maybe he liked to listen to jazz; better than alpine music. She imagined herself standing on a beach with him at sunset, with a cocktail in her hand, like a movie star. Dancing, making love, day after day. Who can blame her?

WHEN I WAS younger I liked to dress up, put on makeup, and go to parties. All the boys fell in love with me, but I didn't go steady with anyone. The important thing was not to go to bed with them, or else they thought you were theirs for life. I would have liked to know what they were like in bed, how they touched you. But you had to be careful, otherwise people thought you were easy. Sometimes, because of the things that went through my mind, I felt that way too, but I didn't tell anyone. My father used to talk to my mother about that kind of woman.

"Good for a roll in the hay."

He scorned them but desired them. My mother would get nervous and he would reassure her.

"You're the only one for me."

He didn't convince us. We couldn't stop thinking about the other kind of woman, the one who was better in bed than we were.

When I was a girl, I went to parties and I felt beautiful. I didn't look at the boys, only at my rivals. The boys' desire for me erased them.

THE BATHROOM IN the apartment is pleasant. I'm sure the bumpkin downstairs didn't decorate it. When he cooks, I have to close the windows because of the smell. You can just imagine the state of the house; no wonder his wife left him. He has an attractive face and nice eyes, but he looks old.

There are dark circles around my eyes. I don't sleep enough. At the end of the month we'll go to the beach. I want to sunbathe. In the morning I'll leave the baby with my mother and Mario and I will go out on the boat.

AFTER WE MET, Mario came to see me at the beach. We used to take the boat out, drop the anchor, and kiss. One time we made love under a beach towel. Then we jumped into the water, sweaty and hot, our heads spinning. We no longer knew who we were, our bodies belonged to the sea.

My mother used to say he was like a rooster in a henhouse. My sister's boyfriend didn't visit, so she left him. At first she waited, and then that was it, she didn't care anymore. Mario enjoyed being the only man in our midst: three sisters and my mother.

My father came on the weekends. He would look at him and laugh: "Ah, you're like a pasha with your harem."

Mario ate with us but slept in a rented room by the port; my mother wouldn't let him stay in the house. In the evening we would tell everyone we were going to the movies and then run to his room to make love. I didn't go to parties. I was afraid that I would never fall in love and that people would call me a whore. One night, a boy said something to me, and it stayed inside, like a brand on a cow in the field.

"You're an *allumeuse*, Marina."

"What do you mean?"

"You're a tease."

One of those nights in his room near the port, I got pregnant. We decided to get married. If I close my eyes, I know why I married him. Not because of the baby, but because of the way he held the rudder of the boat and the way he made love to me. Everything changed with the baby. I wasn't as strong and capable as he expected. But now I'm better: I came here by myself, and at night on the phone I tell him that everything is OK. One month in the mountains by myself. After this, he will trust me and I will once again become the woman he married.

A QUICK LOOK out the window: oh no; the landlord is standing next to the stroller. I didn't hear the car arrive. The baby is awake.

I run downstairs. He stares at me. He is tanned. He must have walked up the mountain today. His face is covered with wrinkles, his eyes are pale and hard, and he speaks in a low voice.

"He undid the straps. It's dangerous to leave him like that, the street is right there."

The baby stares at him and holds his breath.

I mutter, "Thank you. He was asleep so I decided to go up and make his lunch." I pick up the baby.

He turns away. "Good-bye."

He goes into his apartment. His boots are muddy and he smells of sweat and onion. The baby watches him until he disappears, then starts to whimper. I talk to him as we climb the stairs, to calm him.

"Now we'll eat our lunch. Let's hope the soup didn't spill out of the pot! First we'll change and take a bath, and then we'll eat. Are you hungry, my darling?"

JUST LISTEN TO her talking to him on the stairs, the fool. "Are you hungry, darling? You took a nice nap, good for you . . ."

What if he had gotten out of the stroller and walked out into the street? She was cooking his lunch! What a fool. Then if something bad happens, they cry.

Luna used to do everything. Did she ever need help? And she never complained. If I were this woman's husband I wouldn't leave her alone with the baby. She's not up to it, you can tell just from the way she holds him and talks to him. She's really talking to herself, to keep herself calm. Well, it's her husband's problem. It's no business of mine.

I close the door and place my ice axe against the corner of the fireplace, and then take off my shoes.

Tonight I'm going into town to visit my father. I won't tell him, that way maybe the woman will be there and I'll see who it is. We get soft in our old age and end up in some woman's arms. He never needed one before.

That woman upstairs is the type that grabs hold of you when you're young and then you're stuck with her for life. From a good family, raised to be idle. First you have to woo her, then you have to marry her. Now, with the kid, she's stuck. Her husband sent her up here so he could have some peace, poor idiot. He should come and check on her on the weekends.

No breasts, a child's face. She looks at you and you think that it might be fun to take her to bed. You'd hold down her wrists and do whatever you wanted, and she'd like it too.

If the woman from the wood shop isn't willing, I'll have to find someone else. Masturbating while I think about Luna's breasts is enough for a while. But then you need a pussy; there's no replacing it, and that's the point, the crux of the problem.

4

THE PIAZZA IS filled with people and stands. The band plays rustic waltzes and mazurkas and the old people dance. The young people watch them, laughing. I bought a flowered dirndl with a white blouse and apron. And a pair of lederhosen for the boy. We look like two locals, even though I'm not blond with blue eyes and pale skin. I'm the only dark one in the family. My father says I look like his brother who died young.

"MARINA'S EYES ARE just like Sandro's, dark as coal."

Families always repeat the same words, even when it comes to describing who resembles whom. This uncle never married and constantly changed girlfriends. He was a builder and had more money than my father, who worked in a bank and had three daughters.

He used to bring us expensive presents: watches, necklaces, bracelets, rings.

My father scolded him. "You spend all your money . . . What will you do when business is down?"

"Your daughters will help me, won't you?"

We all screamed "Yes!" in unison. I lived in constant hope that my mother would let us wear one of the necklaces or rings to school, to make our friends green with envy. But she would always put away his expensive presents, for "safekeeping."

"You can wear it when you're older," she'd say.

"Can I wear the turquoise necklace, Mamma?"

My uncle would hold it up to my neck.

"You look like a gypsy," he'd say.

And he loved to sing:

Marina, Marina, Marina . . .
Ti voglio al più presto sposar.
Oh mia bella mora, no non mi lasciare,
Non mi devi rovinare . . .

(Marina, Marina, Marina . . .
I want you for my wife.
Oh my brown-haired beauty,
Please don't ever leave me . . .)

My father would glance over with a worried look.

"You're just like your uncle. Let's hope it's only a physical resemblance."

The jewelry was stolen by a burglar one summer when we were away at the beach. We never got to wear any of it. Uncle Sandro died of a heart attack when business turned sour. I always think of both things at once; my father was right about one, and I was right about the other. We should have enjoyed the presents while we had them; I should have worn the turquoise necklace and matching eye shadow and gone dancing.

I cross the piazza with the stroller and look distractedly at the merchandise on display. Cheese, salami, honey, local products. Around here they only sell food, wooden sculptures, loden, and Tyrolese clothing. At night they drink and go to bed early. It's all the same to me; I can't go out because of the baby.

The men stare; there aren't many gypsies around here. I wonder if my landlord is here too? I doubt it. Even the town fair is too worldly for a man who grew up in a mountain lodge.

Women like to tempt fate; otherwise why would anyone marry a man like that and have two children with him? Later, his wife must have realized that he stank of onions and sweat, that he didn't talk and that all he did was climb up and down the mountain. She probably cried at night and dreamt of when she was a girl and men courted her, asked her to dance and to go sailing. But that's me, and Mario is anything but a bumpkin. He's a thinking man, courteous with women, even gallant. He can talk to my father about anything and he's brilliant at what he does.

I could have had a career, but my female colleagues couldn't stand me. They said I dressed provocatively and wanted to impress the boss. It's not true: I studied, graduated with honors, and was a whiz at accounting. I could read a balance sheet faster than any of them and I was pretty, so they hated me. Then the baby was born, and that was the end of it. How they complimented me when I announced I was pregnant!

"How wonderful!"

I was no longer in the way.

The baby turns around in his stroller and stares up at me. Why doesn't he speak? I'm afraid of his silence, it feels like a reproach.

"We'll sit down in a minute, darling, and I'll take you out of there. You'll be able to walk. Don't get upset."

He's quiet today, busy looking at the musicians and the stands. Last night he didn't sleep. He cried so much that I almost lost my mind, like that Sunday.

THAT DAY, HE didn't want to eat and he wouldn't stop crying. He cried in my arms, in his crib, sitting on the floor. He cried if I talked to him or if I tried to get him to play. He was ten months old, and he didn't understand words. What could I do? Mario was working in the living room and I didn't want to bother him. The baby's cries traveled from my ears to my brain; my heart was pounding, and I clenched my fists. He'll stop, just calm down. If he keeps on like this, Mario will come; he'll think that I don't know how to calm the baby.

"Shut up!"

Suddenly the cries stopped; the air was perfectly still, as if I were underwater. His mouth was open but nothing came out, and his nose was running. I was in a cave, surrounded by icy silence. All I could see were hazy spots. There was a light in the distance; then it disappeared. Were my eyes closed? Had I covered my ears? I don't know.

I saw the baby on the floor and Mario picking him up.

"What did you do?"

His words broke the silence. He repeated himself, stammering. I came out of the darkness and into the blinding light. My whole body ached.

"Nothing, I swear! I don't know how he fell."

I started to cry. The baby was calm. He put his head on his father's shoulder. They were both on the same side, hating me.

I took the baby from his arms, hugged him, and talked to him through my tears. A hoarse voice emerged from the darkness and the silence. "I turned around for an instant to grab a diaper, and he fell."

Mario's eyes stared at me, full of hatred. The baby put his arms around my neck and fell asleep. He had exhausted himself crying. I loved him more than anything in the world. How could I make Mario understand?

He is well educated, intelligent, kind ... We went sailing and he rented a room by the harbor. Why did he want to be with me? He wanted to change me ... he knew what I was. This was the real Mario, the one standing here, full of hatred. Go ahead, do it, I thought. "What are you thinking, Mario?" I whispered so as not to wake the baby.

He stared at me a few moments longer, then looked away. "Nothing. You have to be careful! Don't take your eyes off him."

Silently, I reflected.

You're afraid to say it, aren't you? What a trap you've walked into! What kind of woman have you married? Keep your hands off my son. You don't know anything about us. You're the outsider here.

The moment passed. Everything passes and is forgotten, luckily for me. It will never happen again, never. Finally, we looked at each other like two human beings again; we were able to move on from that hatred. I'm normal, I know how to take care of your son, don't worry.

I WALK THROUGH the piazza with the stroller, feeling beautiful and invincible.

My landlord is there, sitting at a table drinking beer with another man. He has cleaned himself up; he's wearing a checkered shirt, ironed—and the usual trousers. His hair is clean and he looks like a normal human being.

"Good day."

"Good day."

Just look at her, dressed up like a fool.

"Stefan, my brother. This is my tenant."

So this is the younger brother, the one with all the girlfriends.

"Hello, I'm Marina."

"Stefan."

They stare at me but don't ask me to sit down, so I decide to say something.

"What a lovely fair."

The bumpkin answers without looking up: "It's always the same."

What can you expect from a man like that? Better leave him alone. The girl at the bakery was right.

"Well, good-bye then."

"Good-bye."

WHAT A NAME, Marina. But she has nice legs. I couldn't tell before, because she always wears trousers. A little on the thin side, but shapely. She ran away; we scared her. Stefan is staring after her; the women from around here aren't enough for him. Now he'll ask me what I think of her, as he always does, ever since he was thirteen.

"So, what do you think?"

"No breasts."

"Manfred, you're obsessed! What's her husband like?"

"I don't know. I don't pay attention to the rental, or to who stays there."

"But you're happy to take the money . . . If Luna hadn't decorated the place, you'd never have been able to rent it. When the carpenter lived there, it was a mess. She wants to make friends."

"Who?"

"Your tenant. She's looking around."

"All women do that. Luna was a champ at scanning her surroundings. She knew how to listen. She knew everybody's business."

"Luna was a beautiful woman."

He's saying it just to get under my skin.

"You should have married her. You would have left her at the altar. How many girlfriends have you had, Stefan?"

"At least I'm the one who leaves them."

Ah, brothers. And to think I raised him.

He was the youngest. I washed his behind and his face every morning. I bundled him up before we went out into the snow. He was always cold. In the snowcat, when we drove down into the valley, I used to wipe his nose with the sleeve of my jacket, so the kids wouldn't call him a snot-nose and tease him because he didn't have a mother.

Albert sat in the front with our father. He never spoke to Stefan. He hated him, and one night he explained why.

"If he hadn't been born, she wouldn't have left."

I used to draw the mountains and the sun for Stefan on a corner of misted-up glass in the snowcat where Albert and my father couldn't see. Albert was right, it was his fault. But how can you know that when you're three?

For three months, he asked for his mother every morning. For three months I didn't say anything. I tried, but I couldn't find the words. The night after father burned all the photographs, I said to him, "If you ask me again, I'll hit you, hard."

That was the last time.

NOW HE TORMENTS me whenever he can.

"You don't understand, Stefan. I made her life impossible, that's why she left."

"Dad said the same thing about our mother, to try to make himself feel stronger. It's better to leave them, before they get the chance."

"Fun game."

"Why don't you ask her to dance, Manfred? Maybe she'll say yes."

She is sitting in a corner of the piazza, but I refuse to turn around. I don't want her to think we're drooling after her.

"I've never danced in my whole life, not even at my own wedding. And she's a complete fool."

"You're a bear, Manfred. Luna was right to leave you."

Stefan turns around again to look at her. "Look at her, she's dancing by herself."

This time I turn around.

She's dancing with her little boy. She squeezes him and he laughs. She holds his head next to hers and sways, turns, and rocks this way and that. The baby is drooling with excitement. People are looking at her; that's what she wants.

ONE CHRISTMAS, UP at the lodge, my mother picked me up and danced with me. Then she started to sing. Her face, her dark eyes, the smell of her hair. The room and the candles spun around me. My father sat, watching us. She's mine now, I've stolen her from him. Whore. Just like this woman. If a woman is happy, you should worry. When they run in the snow or kiss you and caress you with tears in their eyes, you should run, as fast as you can.

STEFAN WATCHES HER with his mouth open, poor fool. There is some beer foam on his whiskers. He looks like his mother but he doesn't know it. He's never seen her, not even in a photograph.

"What's wrong, Stefan, are you in a trance?"

"A woman who dances with her baby like that must be a fool."

"What have I been telling you?"

5

IT'S BEEN RAINING for two days. Each morning we go out for a walk and then turn around and come back inside. The baby has a cold; his nose is stuffy and he can't breathe. The pharmacist gave me some homeopathic drops, but they're useless. Back in the city, I give him antihistamines at night, even though the pediatrician says I shouldn't. "The only physiological solution is to give him an extra pillow so he can breathe more easily."

An extra pillow? That way he wouldn't sleep at all. These silly mountain folk won't sell me antihistamines without a prescription. We haven't slept in two nights. Now the minute I sit down, I start to drift off. I have to pay attention; he's attracted to light sockets. He also likes to climb onto the wood chest; he knocks over vases, plates, anything and everything. Toys don't interest him.

"Mamma, go away!"

He's determined to do as he pleases.

I'm on my third coffee. I have to stay awake until eight, and it's only five. It's raining steadily, and there's no one outside. The shops are closed because it's Sunday. Nothing to do until evening, not even a bath, because of his cold. And the house isn't heated. He's always so happy in the bath, and then I can relax.

"We'll go swimming at the beach. You'll love it! I'll buy you an inflatable raft and we'll row around with Daddy."

When I say the word "Daddy" he stops and stares. He misses Mario. When Mario calls, he listens and then turns away. He hands me the phone. He doesn't want to talk.

I talk to him while he plays in the bath, to calm him but also because I think he's old enough now to understand what I'm saying.

ON THE ISLAND there's a beach where the sand is so hot you could fry an egg on it. Three black rocks rise out of the water, which is as calm as a lake. I used to go swimming there with my sisters until late in the afternoon. The red, liquid sun would sink into the sea, and then we would scream and yell and dive into the golden ribbons of dying light. The water was like hot ink, and my mother would call out to us, towels in hand.

"Marina, come here! You're the last one, as usual."

"I'LL NEVER MAKE you get out of the water unless you want to. You love the water, so you'll be a good swimmer. But

I can't give you a bath tonight, because of your cold. No, don't climb up there, it's dangerous! You'll fall."

"Mamma, no!"

"Stop that! You can't go there, there are bottles and you'll hurt yourself. Don't cry, come on, let's play a game. Let's play with blocks. We'll build a tower and then you can knock it down. I can see you're not interested . . . Why do you have to climb up on that? Look, there's nothing there for you, just two wine bottles, a bottle of oil, the salt and pepper shakers, the sugar bowl, the coffee jar.

It's good wine. I don't scrimp on wine. I don't smoke, I don't go out, but I like to have a drink in the evenings. Yesterday I drank almost a whole bottle. I mustn't tell Mario, or he'll think I have a problem, on top of everything else. Wine helps me relax, it warms me up inside, and I don't feel so lonely and tired.

"Get down from there! Good boy. Play with your toy cars."

Vroom vroom. He calms down for a bit. That way I can think for a few minutes. A minute is already something, sixty seconds, a long time. I have to use my minutes well, but then it's so difficult to pull myself out of my thoughts. Sit down, Marina, take advantage of this moment, you can clean up later.

My mind wanders. How wonderful it is to think! When you're young you don't realize it. On Sunday mornings you can stay in bed and daydream as long as you please. In class, you listen, dream, sleep. How lucky you were, but of course you didn't enjoy it to the fullest. One should never miss an occasion to think! Ever since the baby was born, you've become aware of how precious time is. At cafés and in the street, people walk, smoke, and converse, carefree and unaware, with no sense of haste. They have all the time in the world. They don't realize how lucky they are. I push the baby stroller; once I too was like them.

In the fall I'll go back to work, part-time. I'll leave him with my mother in the mornings. I'll have to take him to her because she doesn't go out early in the morning. Before eight o'clock; it will be cold. How long before he gets sick? When he does, I won't be able to go to work. If I hire someone, she'll have to come every morning and it will be too expensive.

Mario doesn't understand.

"Why don't you ask for leave until he can go to day care? After all, your salary isn't very large."

I'll never be able to get an important position now, but at least they pay you to think, what a privilege! If I can't go to work for part of the day, I'll go crazy. I know that other women don't feel this way; they suffer when they have to leave their child to go to work. My sister quit her job to be a full-time mother. She said: "It was hell. At home all I could think about was the office, and at the office all I could think about was home. This is the life I want."

But now she's always tense and bosses everyone around. Maybe the same will happen to me and I'll end up wanting to stay home, but now all I can dream about is the office.

In the corner of sky I can make out from my office I can see seagulls and swallows in the spring. I have my own computer, my pens, my paper. There's a balance sheet to read, a report to write. Hours of quiet work ahead of me. At one we go for lunch at the café and tell each other stories about our lives. And we laugh, how we laugh . . .

"WHERE ARE YOU? No, don't go there! Why do you want to climb up there? Look, here's your truck! You didn't know it was there, did you? It was hidden under the table. There, there, that's a good boy."

I wonder why boys are drawn to cars, from the very beginning. Now's he's in the truck, driving around like a madman down a road full of twists and turns. He's bold, fearless, and then boom, he crashes into the wall and the truck rolls over, but he's not afraid. He gets right up and keeps going, driving around like a madman . . . I love to watch him play.

MY SISTER AND I used to play with dolls, but she was better at it than I was. I didn't enjoy dressing them up, preparing their food, cleaning the house. She would send me off to do the food shopping. The flowers were vegetables, ivy leaves were steaks, wisteria was grapes, little sticks were knives and forks, bark became plates. She would say, "You're the husband. You go out and gather food for us."

I wasn't happy with that; I wanted a husband too, but there was no arguing with her, she was older and she got to decide.

"You're too distracted to be a good wife."

So I played the husband, knowing that one day I would get to play the wife. But she was right; my head is in the clouds, I've always been that way.

The teacher used to say to my mother, "Marina is a dreamer."

I'm not sure it was a compliment. Sometimes it seemed like a good thing. I would meet a boy and he would stare at me and ask, "What are you thinking about?"

"Lots of things," I would say.

And he would be intrigued because he wanted to know, in detail.

But it made my father angry.

"What are you thinking about?"

He wanted me to pay attention when he tried to explain math problems. I would get distracted and nervous. I lost count of how long he had been talking, and I wondered whether he had asked me a question. What did he want to know? I needed time to think, and I didn't realize that time had passed and he was beginning to lose patience.

Where is it that my thoughts go? The world stands still, and I wander around, observing people, playing tricks on them. It's fun, and time passes quickly, but then it turns out your time is up.

"You forgot to buy potatoes," my sister would say. She never forgot.

I HEAR A loud thud—what happened?

The wine bottles are on the floor, and there's oil every-where . . . The baby is crying, surrounded by broken glass. My

God, he's hurt! Is that blood or wine? What have you done? Don't cry! Oil and wine are spreading across the floor and blending together. The kitchen is full of liquid, like a sinking boat; the liquid spreads toward the living room. It smells like a tavern. I'll have to mop it up, but when, how? Where do I put him? I can't put him to bed, he'll climb out.

I pick him up and slip on the oil. We sit on the floor amid the broken glass, like two shipwrecked souls. His head is bleeding and so is my leg. He's crying now. He won't stop.

"Mamma, go away!"

I can't handle it, he's right. I wasn't born for this; it's been wrong from the beginning. Rage! Rivers of incandescent rage. I can't hold them back any longer. I'm full of hate. Mario, my mother, my father, my sisters . . . They can all go to hell! I want to die here with him, on this floor stinking of oil and wine. I'd like to close my eyes here with him.

Come darkness, cold, silence. Save us both from this disaster. Come and take me, I've been waiting for you. Make this crying animal be silent, he's killing me. I scream.

"*Basta!* Be quiet! Quiet! Stop it!"

That's it. Good. He's not crying anymore. It's finished. Finally some quiet.

WHAT ARE THOSE two doing up there? The baby is crying and she's screaming. Objects falling on the floor, banging. What has she broken? I'll make her pay for it. They should take babies away from their mothers the moment they're born, just as my father said.

It's none of my business how people raise their children. The earlier they grow up and leave home, the better. I became a mountain guide so I could leave home. I'd rather not be indoors any more than necessary. I sleep three hours, get up, and walk out into the night.

With Luna and the kids it wasn't possible. I allowed myself to get trapped in a prison. But it was she who complained, "You've locked me up in a prison." And I would respond, "Do you realize what I did for you? I locked myself up in a house. And now you want to go out, eat in restaurants, go to the city? No, that's too easy. We'll stay here, together in our trap, with our beautiful children."

It's too quiet now. I can't hear anything at all. Maybe they've gone to bed. But it's only six, it's too early. After her idiotic scream, a dead silence. No child quiets down that quickly. Something must have happened. I'll go and listen. I'll go upstairs quietly, and if I hear them I'll turn back.

On the stairs, silence. I can't hear either of them. Something must have happened. I ring the doorbell. It's my house, I'm responsible.

No answer. I try again. Silence.

"Do you hear me?! Answer the door!"

Silence.

"Open up!"

I yell and bang on the door.

Silence. I look down and see liquid seeping under the door. I lean down and smell it. Wine.

A broken bottle. What happened? I have to knock down the door. I run to get the ice axe next to the fireplace and back up the stairs. I aim it at the lock and try to break it. Neither she nor the baby make any sound, as if they can't hear me. Something serious must have happened. Maybe they're dead. I strike the lock again, three or four times.

The wood splinters but doesn't break. It's a solid door. A carpenter used to live here; he must have reinforced it. I'll try again, harder. It can't be harder than rock. Finally, a hole, now I just have to make it bigger. Big enough for my hand. I unlock the door from the inside and open it.

The light is on and the floor is wet. The room with the fireplace is empty. In the kitchen, the baby is on the floor with his eyes closed, lying amid broken glass and liquid. Blood? I pick him up, he's breathing. There is blood on his head. Where is she? I move slowly, careful not to slip with the baby in my arms. There she is behind a door, curled up on the floor like a pile of rags.

"What happened?"

Her eyes are empty.

"Can you hear me? Wake up!"

I should slap her, but my hands are full. I kick her.

"Get up!"

Now she's trembling, like Luna. She does as I say.

"Did he fall?"

She doesn't answer. I hand her the child.

"Hold his head, talk to him. Try to wake him."

She takes him in her arms without looking. She says nothing, awaiting orders.

"Let's go."

6

DARKNESS. TREES, A bridge, twists and turns, a dark stream. Who is driving? Where am I? The baby is sleeping. Where are we going? He fell and hit his head. I hold him close. My God, why doesn't he wake up?

The landlord is driving. We are in his car. Where is he taking us? How did he get in? I hear his hard voice, whispering.

"Did he fall asleep again?"

He stares at me in the rearview mirror.

"Yes."

"Talk to him, wake him up. What's his name?"

"Marco."

Why does she have that haunted look? What is she afraid of?

"We're almost there. He shouldn't fall back asleep. Wake him, talk to him!"

"My darling, wake up! Come on, sit up."

"Don't move him!"

"Don't sleep, my love, open your eyes, look at Mamma."

She's crying now, the fool.

"Keep going, speak louder."

"Everything is all right, my love. Wake up, I beg you! Now we'll see the doctor and he'll make everything all right. Open your eyes, look at Mamma! I'm here, near you, I won't leave you!"

What have I done? Mario mustn't know.

"Don't console him, let him cry. It's better if he cries. And you, stop crying! You're not a child!"

Bastard.

"Did he hit his head?"

Don't tell him anything, Marina. Be careful. I mutter, "He climbed up onto the table and slipped, taking the bottles with him."

"Where did he hit his head?"

"I'm not sure."

"Where were you?"

The fool, why does she look down? "I said, don't move him! Let him cry, it's good for him. Caress him, but without moving him. Where were you?"

"In the bathroom. I only left him for an instant."

Why did I say that? I should have said I was there but didn't make it in time to stop him.

She's lying. Why was she sitting behind the door instead of with the child, holding him in her arms?

"You could have put him in his crib."

"He climbs out of it. He was playing nicely with his cars, so I thought I'd have enough time to go to the bathroom."

"Why were you behind the door instead of with him?"

Bastard. I won't answer.

"Stop crying, we're here. Take him in, and I'll park."

A driveway, patches of light on a lawn, flowers, empty benches. Emergency room entrance. Two nurses come out to meet us.

I must repeat the same thing to everyone: he climbed up on the table and slipped, bringing down the bottles with him. He hit his head hard.

The nurses open the door.

"What happened?"

"He climbed on the kitchen table and slipped, taking the bottles down with him. He hit his head hard."

"We'll take him in for observation."

"Can I come? He'll get scared if he doesn't see me."

"No, we'll call you."

He begins to scream. They take him from me. I want to die.

I FOLLOW THEM until they disappear behind a glass door. The waiting room is empty except for a mother with her newborn. It's clean, with pictures of happy children on the walls.

I sit down to keep from crumpling to the floor. The mother stares at me. I look away, but I know she will ask me.

"Did he fall?"

"Yes."

She smiles. "With my firstborn, I was always at the emergency room. Boys never stop moving."

What have I done? I feel like I'm about to start screaming. Stop, Marina. No one knows what happened. They'll be able to fix him. He'll be scared without me. I should have gone with him, held him. What harm would it have done? Maybe he won't want me to hold him anymore.

Mamma, go away!

I cry, and everything grows cloudy: the waiting room, the empty chairs, the pictures of happy children.

"Don't cry. Children are strong."

What does she know? What does anyone know about me? No one knows. The bastard suspects something. Where did he go? I have to get rid of him. If he comes back I'll thank him and tell him to go home. I can manage on my own. The only thing that matters is that the baby is OK and no one knows. Mario. My mother. Otherwise, they'll take him away. And if they take him, I'll kill myself. There he is.

"Where is the boy?"

"They took him inside."

I get up, so he gets the message.

"Thank you for everything. I'm going to stay here with him, but you should go home."

Now she plays the grande dame, but she won't get rid of me that easily.

"Let's see how he's doing first. The police will want to talk to me."

My legs are shaking. I'd better sit.

This man hates me. He wants me dead. I must be stronger, and more clever. Marina, get a hold of yourself, think things through, stop crying. Act like an adult. You must protect your baby and get rid of this bastard.

I smile at him. My eyes are still moist; maybe he'll feel sorry for me.

"I'm sorry about how I behaved before. I was confused. I saw him lying on the floor, bloody, with his eyes closed, and I was terribly afraid, so I hid behind the door like a child."

The woman with the newborn interrupts.

"It happens. When my son used to fall I would cover my face so as not to see him. I couldn't help it. My husband always went."

I smile at her, then at him, without a word.

Nothing to say?

IT'S POSSIBLE. SHE hid behind the door because she's a fool, like they all are. Like Luna, when Clara fell off the bike and broke her arm. She was frozen, terrified, and clutched her face with her hands. I yelled at her to help me, and then she started to follow instructions like an automaton, just like this one. But why is she so afraid of me, and why does she want to get rid of me? There is blood on her leg.

I GET UP and go to the door. Why hasn't he come out yet? Let me see him, please. God, let him be all right. I sit down again.

How could I? What part of me did this? It's like the other time, with Mario. I let him fall off the bed. No, he fell all by himself. It happened to my mother with one of us. Maybe this time, too, it's not my fault. He climbed up on the table, he fell, he hit his head, and I thought it was my fault. In any case it's still my fault because I was distracted.

The dark cloud, the crying that won't stop, it all makes your head spin. I did it, I banged him against the table, I hurt my baby. It's not possible. I love him more than anything in the world. Ever since he was born, I've never left him in anyone else's care. I'm sleep-deprived, it's true, but I don't complain. I miss my freedom, but he'll grow up and I'll be able to go out, work, go to the movies. What am I thinking? He's in there, alone, and this is what I think about! What are they doing to him? Why doesn't my baby come out of there?

THIS WOMAN IS not telling the truth. First the noise, the clatter of falling objects, the baby crying. All normal: the baby climbs on the table, knocks over the bottles, slips, and cries. But then her scream, a loud bang, and total silence. Not a sound emerges from inside the house. I break down the door and she doesn't react. The child is on the floor, lying in the midst of broken glass, and she doesn't pick him up. She's not telling the truth, it didn't happen as she says.

THE DOOR OPENS and a nurse emerges. I go up to him. He asks, "Are you the mother?"

"Yes, how is he?"

"He's awake. We put in some stitches, and now we'll do a CAT scan. We'll keep him under observation overnight. You can see him now."

"Let me just say good-bye to the man who brought us here."

He's on his feet, watching us. He has the face of an old man and the body of a much younger one, with the same droopy trousers he always wears, the same plaid shirt and sandals. The nurse approaches him.

"Did you find them?"

"Yes."

"On your way, you should stop by the police to give your statement."

A statement? Oh no, what will he say? I smile at him. Be nice!

"Thank you for driving us here."

"You're welcome."

"Hopefully, I'll be back tomorrow."

"Do I need to inform anyone?"

"No, thank you. My husband is easily alarmed. It's better if I tell him."

What a husband.

"Let me know how the boy does."

"Of course. Good night."

"Good night."

He doesn't know a thing. What does he suspect? He didn't see anything.

THIS LONG, EMPTY, blue hallway must have terrified him. And all these faces. He's afraid of the pediatrician, imagine all these nurses. We go into a room.

There he is. He's playing with a little box in the crib. Poor darling, his head is all bandaged up. He wants me to pick him up in my arms. He doesn't remember anything.

"Hello, my love, what are you doing? Are you playing with that box?"

I swallow my tears. I mustn't cry.

"They put a bandage on your head. How do you feel?"

"He'll be fine. Marco is a strong little man, and very brave."

The doctor is a woman. She stares at me sternly, or perhaps I'm only imagining it. Marina, be calm.

"Who told you his name?"

"He did. How old is he?"

"Two in September."

"I asked him where he fell."

My heart jumps. I must keep calm. She mustn't know.

"And what did he say?"

"From the truck."

Joy. I laugh.

"Before he climbed up on the table, he was playing with his toy truck. He was behaving so well that I thought I could leave him alone for a moment to pee. Then I heard a terrible crash . . . He had climbed up on the table and knocked over all the bottles, and then he fell on the broken glass . . . I can't leave him alone, not even for a moment."

I feel her watching me. I'm afraid she senses something.

"They call them 'the terrible twos.'"

"I'm sorry?"

"The terrible twos. They don't know how to play by themselves, but they never stop moving, and they don't sleep because they're afraid of everything. Mine was the same."

Relief, calm. Mine was the same, she says. Perhaps even she has lost control at times. After all, what did I do? A moment of rage; maybe he hit his head when he fell and I didn't realize it.

"Can I pick him up?"

She nods. I pull him toward me and kiss him.

"So, you tell the doctor everything but you won't talk to me?"

"Now we'll do a CAT scan."

I shudder.

"We gave him six stitches."

"Six! But there's nothing wrong? I mean, on the inside?"

"I don't think so. He's very alert."

The world is light, the hospital is a paradise. I could hug this woman. She has saved my life.

"We'll do the CAT scan, and then we'll take you to the pediatrics floor."

I begin to cry. "Thank you."

She puts a hand on my shoulder. "Is he the first?"

"Yes."

"Babies fall. Sometimes it can even be an opportunity for growth."

7

⌒

THE MOUNTAIN REAPPEARS from behind the rain and clouds, in a shimmering light. The colors are bright, the meadow is wet with rain. The cows are filling their bellies with wet grass. My clients canceled. After a week of uninterrupted rain, they didn't believe the sun would come out. I told them: "Tomorrow will be sunny. We'll be able to go up to the lodge."

It was no good. They left, but I insisted on being paid anyway.

The woman came back from the hospital the next day. We crossed paths in the entryway. She was carrying the boy, his head wrapped in bandages. She smiled at me. Now she's gentle and attentive.

"Thank you again. What would I have done without you! The CAT scan results were good. They'll remove the stitches in five days."

The following morning I could hear her talking on the phone with her husband as she sat on the bench in front of the house. The baby was sleeping in his stroller.

"He's fine, I promise. You don't need to come. He fell. You know how it is, he's never still, not even for a moment."

He must be one of those men who believe everything their wives tell them without batting an eye. I can understand. You don't want trouble with your wife. You sacrifice your kids and wash your hands of the problem.

That night after the hospital, I stopped by the police station. They greeted me with pats on the back and jokes.

"Ciao, Manfred, how are you? It's been a while since your last visit."

The last time was after Luna went to the hospital, the night I hit her.

WE HAD BEEN arguing for months.

"The kids aren't allowed to watch TV, and you take them up the mountain every Sunday! They want to be with their friends! They're grown up!"

We argue about the children, but really we're fighting about us. I can't stand her, her moods, her constant desire to try new things, fix up the house, buy knickknacks. At night her tits fill me with desire. I don't think about her face or her voice but about her body. Luna is willing, but not enthusiastic. She doesn't like anything about me anymore. She married me, but now she scoffs at everything I say or do. Even the sex.

That day she got under my skin, yelling about something or other.

I stopped to think for a moment. Look how she attacks you. She's not afraid of you, she doesn't respect you. She feels stronger because you still want her.

So I hit her.

"THOSE DAYS ARE over, Manfred. You're not allowed to hit your wife anymore."

The officers laugh. They'd like to do it too.

"Luna doesn't want to press charges, but don't do it again. It didn't work out well for your father; it wasn't easy to grow up with him on your own."

If your mother leaves you, you're marked for life. If your wife leaves you and keeps the children, it's just one of those things. I asked Luna to let me keep the kids.

"They can live with me. I want them. My father raised us on his own. And after all, I'm not the one who's leaving."

"That way they'll grow up crazy like you. Don't push me. When they're small, they always give the children to their mother. They'll come and see you from time to time."

"Thank you."

I TELL THE police what I heard in the apartment upstairs. The scream, the thud, and the sudden silence. And what I saw when I entered the apartment.

"You have a grudge against women, Manfred. You can't

stand them. First your mother, then Luna. We understand. But they're not all bad. Your father was unlucky, but Luna was all right. You're a difficult man, Manfred. Just go home. You did the right thing."

What a compliment. Just like what my father said, after the wedding: "Congratulations, now you're married."

It takes courage to get married and it takes courage to bash in a door when it's too quiet inside.

THAT DAY ON the bench, after she finished her phone call with her husband, she walked up to me. I knew what she wanted to ask.

"How did it go with the police statement?"

"Fine."

"Did they ask you any questions?"

That night, I used the more casual *tu*, but now I've reverted to the more formal *lei*.

"Yes, they always do after an accident."

How sweet the little mamma is! Everything is fine, everyone is OK. Who are you kidding? I'll make you talk. But it's better if she thinks everything is all right. That way she'll let down her guard. Just look at that smile!

"Someday I'd like to go up to your brother's lodge. I've heard it's beautiful there, and one can take the lift and then hike up a path that's not too strenuous. Could I do it with the baby?"

Women always walk right into the mouth of the wolf. They have an instinct for trouble. I shouldn't offer my services right away.

"It's easy. I take my clients, even the ones who aren't big walkers. Do you hike?"

"Not really."

I knew it. I'll take you up there, that way we'll have time to talk. You'll never make it to the top. I'll take you to the forest, up the steepest shortcut, over the moraine and the Gola della Dama peak. We'll see how long you last.

"You'll have to carry the boy on your back. Do you have equipment?"

"Unfortunately, no. If my husband had come, we would have bought a pack, but by myself . . ."

"I have one that we used to use for the kids when they were little."

"Thank you! That's very kind."

How could I ever have thought this mountain man suspected me? He doesn't talk much but he's not mean. And he minds his own business.

"Anyway, it's nice up there. I grew up there."

"Maybe we could go after he gets his stitches removed."

TODAY IS THE day. A group of climbers canceled at the last minute, so I've been paid. The boy is well, and he's no longer wearing bandages. The sun is out. I'll go up and see if she wants to come.

Karl from the wood shop nailed a piece of plywood over the hole in the door. When her husband arrives I'll tell him he has to pay for a new door. He doesn't have time to come when his son falls; he must work a lot and make good money.

She comes to the door with the baby in her arms, her hair messy and loose. She's surprised, and maybe a little bit scared.

"Hello."

"Hello. I'm going up to the lodge this morning. If you want you can come too, that way I can help you."

What do I do? The bumpkin remembered. A whole day with him? No, I don't think I can stand it.

"Maybe it's a bit tiring for the baby."

"As you like, but I won't ask again."

He starts to leave without saying good-bye.

"Wait, let me think. Maybe it'll be good for him. Is it very far?"

How careful she is!

"The path is full of kids. But it's up to you."

"I should buy some food for us."

"I have everything we need. You have ten minutes, while I get ready."

He leaves. What a strange man.

8

WE'RE ON THE gondola. I look down. The altitude frightens me, but I'm also drawn to it. Cliffs, streams, boulders, pylons. The lift shakes each time we overtake a pylon. I look away. The baby is excited; he wants to stick his head through the half-open window. I whisper to him, "Come on, don't do that. You have to stay still. I'll put you down when we get to the top."

He starts to whimper. A group of Austrians stare at us and whisper among themselves. I shouldn't have accepted. The baby will drive everyone crazy, including him. For the time being he doesn't seem annoyed. He has his back to us, and stares out the window. He knows every path, every tree. I bet he has played hide-and-seek in these trees and jumped over the streams with his brothers.

"Calm down, my love, we'll be there soon."

I put his head on my shoulder. He cranes his neck and whines. The bumpkin turns suddenly.

"Quiet."

I start, and the baby hides his face in my shoulder, peering at him out of one eye, in silence. This is the only word he has said in the lift: sharp, dry, and quiet.

Where is he taking us? Up to the lodge. The path is easy and he'll carry the boy on his back.

The green meadows are behind us now and we approach the dark woods, gray masses of thousand-year-old rocks, dusty and precariously balanced above the valley, ready to carry away homes, men, women, children, and cows at any time.

I hold the baby close. I'm drawn to the black boulders and the abyss.

"Marina, come on! You're always the last, and it's getting cold!"

The sea is far away at sunset. The cold here is like the cold inside me; it doesn't frighten me. At the last pylon, I lose my balance and graze his arm. The tartan shirt, always the same, and the smell of his skin. Thin, lean. Like all mountain climbers. Prematurely old men.

SHE CAN BARELY stand on her own two feet! Now I'll take her on a nice walk. The meadow, the uphill path through the woods, the waterfall, the moraine, the path beneath the ice . . . If she doesn't reach the plateau, no lunch! She'll beg for mercy. She'll plead with me to stop, and then she'll tell me the truth, admit what she did to her child. Unnatural, heartless mother. The baby can't even defend himself; he wants you near him no matter what you do to him.

⌒

I WANTED TO be near as well. Is that her?

Footsteps in the snow at night. My father would step out of the lodge to see who was there. He couldn't accept that she was never coming back. He would stay up, waiting for her. Now I know. Until that night I was convinced he had been the one to send her away. That was what he said at first.

"I sent her away. She couldn't live here with us. She wanted us to move into town, and I said no."

I hated him. Why hadn't she taken me with her? I would have hidden away with her, down in the valley, where the roads are straight and smooth, not like here where we have to take the snowcat, struggling through the snow and rocks.

That night I got out of bed with my brothers and we all went downstairs, quietly, in order of seniority: Albert, Manfred, Stefan. Albert's feet were filthy; already back then, he didn't like to bathe. Mother used to scold him.

"Albert, come here and take a bath! Do I have to strip you down?"

Standing in the doorway, we stared at our father. He was crying. Like one of us. Though, it must be said, we never cried in front of him, he didn't allow it. But here he was, crying, with his head on the table. Next to him, a glass of wine, an empty bottle. If our father was crying, anything was possible. Without our shell, we are like slugs, like the ones we used to crush on the path with our boots, always a size too big, so they would last longer. Seeing him like that with his head on the table, I felt like I no longer had a spine, or muscles. I couldn't speak.

Why was he crying, if he sent her away?

I didn't ask Albert. He always said that I didn't understand, that I was dumb. He would tell me, and I would tell Stefan, like a chain. Albert was the eldest, and she had spoken to him the night before she left. I saw them. But he hated her, and never mentioned her. Now we watched him, awaiting an explanation for our father's tears.

"Another man stole his wife."

It took me a few moments to understand. Then, suddenly, it was clear: our mother and "his wife" were the same person. Stole? Who? Did he steal her from us as well? No one at school must know. We're in the same shit, our father and the three of us.

I threw away the bluebells she pressed for me between the pages of a book. They were no use to me. We threw away everything she left behind. My father burned every photograph.

THE GONDOLA JOLTS to a stop. We have arrived. The Austrians get off first. Look how she shivers! She's cold. Just wait! She'll warm up during our walk. I tell her, "It's cold, but you'll be warm once we start walking."

"Shall we let him walk a bit?"

"No, I'll carry him in the backpack."

"He might cry."

"Marco is a mountaineer; he only cries when he's around women, isn't that right?"

He puts the baby in the pack. Marco doesn't make a sound.

"Who told you his name was Marco?"

"He did. Why do you always call him 'the baby'? He has a name. Let's go."

What a bastard. Now he's telling me what to do, like everyone else.

The meadow up here is beautiful. Sun, wet grass. The cows chew happily. They look up as we go by. Marco answers them: "Moo!"

I laugh. "He loves cows. He always does that when he sees them."

The man doesn't react. The Austrian tourists take the path marked "Rifugio della Dama—easy, two hours." Why do we go the other way?

"Aren't we going to the lodge?"

"We're taking a shortcut."

"How far is it? The sign says two hours."

"This way is shorter, if we shut up and walk."

How could his wife stand it? No conversation at all. I bet even in bed he doesn't say a word, just touches and comes, what a bore! As my friend says about her husband: "Some nights when he comes home from work it's like his pants are already undone. It's written all over his face: he wants it."

I'll bet this bumpkin is the same. I'll bet he takes off his shirt and leaves his pants on the floor, so it's easier to put them on again the next day. He barely looks at you, and he's already hard.

"The baby . . . Marco . . . will be hungry soon."

"How soon?"

"About an hour."

"We'll take a break."

I keep my eyes on his shoes ahead of me on the path. For now, it's not too bad, but what about later? I feel out of shape.

I USED TO swim when I was little. We went to the mountains as well, but I always felt cold when we went skiing, and I would fall because I was distracted. I preferred skating, because it was like dancing. There was music and I could lean on a boy to steady myself. I liked to be lifted. I felt light, like I could become part of a boy's body. If he was good, he didn't have to push much, a touch was enough. If only life were like that. Instead, the music ends and then the same boy who seemed so perfect, made for you and you for him, can barely hold a conversation. Mario doesn't like to dance. No boy worth spending time with likes to dance. Why is the world divided between the men who dance and the men you can really fall in love with?

THE BUMPKIN WALKS quickly, effortlessly. It's all he does, after all. He climbs up rock faces and glaciers with ropes. Who knows how many mountains he has climbed. I'd like to ask him about his wife, his children, his brothers. But he doesn't speak. Even so, it's nice of him to bring us here and carry the baby on his back. Marco is asleep. His head bumps against the metal bar of the backpack.

"Wait a minute, let me put something under his head."

He stops without turning around. I pull out Mario's sweater, the one the baby sleeps with, and fold it under his head. Ever since that night, I can't look at him when he has his eyes closed. When he opens them I feel better.

"Done."

He starts walking again. We've just begun, and I'm already tired. Two hours! I'll have to push through the fatigue. I'd rather die than slow down. He leans on his ice axe as he walks.

When the carpenter came to nail two planks over the hole in the door, he was impressed by the damage.

"Manfred really did a number with that axe!"

The following day in the hospital, I reconstructed the series of events. The banging, his screams. I didn't answer; it was as if I weren't there. He broke through the door and found me hiding behind the kitchen door. The baby was on the floor, alone. I wonder what he *really* said to the police?

And now this morning he decides to take me to the lodge. I wonder why? I mentioned the idea a few days ago; I wonder if I should pay him? Yes, it's better, that way I don't owe him anything. Even if he thinks he knows something, he has no proof. And after all, why should he? What does he care? It's none of his business.

We reach the forest. The sun doesn't filter through the branches. The man chops a mushroom with his axe, and it rolls down the slope. It must be poisonous.

"What are these trees?"

"Larches and firs."

"You know the area well."

"I grew up here."

"You have two brothers?"

"Yes."

"No sisters?"

"Luckily."

And not the faintest trace of a mother, I'd like to add; that's why you are the way you are. You barely utter three words, and there's no one waiting for you back home.

"I have two sisters."

"Your poor father."

"He says he's a lucky man, because he has four women to look after him."

"So he says."

I can't stand him. As soon as we get to the lodge, I'll go my own way, of that you can be sure.

"You have two children, don't you?"

"Who told you?"

"Didn't you say you got that backpack for them? And I saw the bicycles back at the house."

"Simon and Clara."

"Beautiful names."

"If you say so."

"How old are they?"

"Ten and seven."

I'm a little frightened to ask about his wife, or why the children don't live with him. But if I don't ask, it will seem like I already know, like I've been asking around.

"They don't live with you?"

"No. They're coming at the end of the month."

I'm out of breath. The bumpkin is going too fast. This path is steep, and I'm getting tired. How much time has gone by? If only Marco would wake up. If he cries, we can stop. But he's sleeping like an angel. He never sleeps this time of day. I'm out of breath. Perhaps it's the altitude.

WE USED TO go for hikes in the mountains. Mamma never came. Our father would line us up and tell stories to make the time pass and help us forget how tired we were.

I would daydream, embroidering on one of his stories and imagining myself as a character in its plot. With a bit of stardust, I could make the others around me disappear one by one, first my father, then my two sisters. I would imagine I was climbing the mountain on my own, that I wasn't afraid of encountering the bear who lived in the cave just around the corner. Under the fur there was a nice man, but first I had to tame him, otherwise he would tear me apart. Under the first layer of fur, there was another, and another; it took hours to strip him down to his skin, even days, centuries. If you weren't careful, he would kill you and you would lie there, in a pool of blood. His claws would carve out parallel furrows in your flesh, then he would bite off a chunk of your cheek and the veins, tendons, and nerves would dangle like electric cords. You could see them hanging outside of your body. Dead. The bear would sniff at the sockets where your eyes once were and the gaping gash in your cheek. Then he would leave you there, and you would just lie on the ground, observing your own body, separated from you forever.

I found many different ways to tell the story; sometimes the girl would have a sword, or she would suddenly become a woman and the story would start over, with a different ending. That way, I didn't feel tired on the way up the mountain, or bored. Boredom is more tiring than hiking.

SHE'S A GOOD walker, I never would have guessed it. With those skinny legs and no muscle. She's all nerves, this one.

I speed up little by little, so she doesn't notice. She stays right behind me. I'm in command here, and she knows it. Only a few people know this path, and we have yet to cross anyone on the trail. But I need a plan. I'll make her walk until the baby wakes up. It will take some time. Clara could sleep for two hours straight in the thin mountain air, lulled by the steady movement. If she walks for two hours at this speed, she'll be exhausted. We'll stop to feed the baby and I'll say something. Not everything, just a little. She'll wonder how much I know. She'll contradict herself and be forced to tell the truth. I'll be like the police, little by little I'll back her into a corner, until there is no way out but the truth.

Why are you doing this, Manfred? To punish her. And because the child is in danger; they should take him away from her. My father was right, women don't know how to raise children. I'll threaten to tell her husband, good idea; that's what she fears the most. She didn't ask him to come and he fell for it. Men don't want to know, they close their eyes. I would have sacrificed Clara and Simon to have Luna with me at night. My father would have given us up to have her back. It wouldn't have been enough.

"Love turns into hate."

My father said that once, when I told him I was getting married. Before.

"Good for you."

Then he started to tell me about what had happened. He hadn't explained anything when I was a kid, and when I was getting married, I didn't want to know. But now that he's an old man, he's different. He has a lady friend in the city. He can keep talking as long as he likes.

"The night before she left, your mother still wanted me. She served tables in the dining room, worked, helped with your homework, bathed you, undressed, and came to bed. We talked about the work that had to be done around the lodge, about the guests. She mentioned the American too. 'He's alone,' she said. 'He doesn't like American women, he finds them fake.' 'Maybe he likes you,' I said."

I interrupted him. "So you knew?"

"I could tell. She barely spoke to him, and never looked him in the eye."

"And you did nothing to stop her?"

"I thought it would pass. I played cards with the American in the evenings. He didn't look at her either. Your mother cleaned the tables, poured our drinks, and went to bed. She said good night, and so did he. They never looked at each other. He came up here to hike, and he knew what he was doing. I went out with him a few times. He said that American mountains were fake. 'Like the women?' I asked. He said yes, laughing. They must have spoken when I was out in the snowcat, because they never did in front of me. 'Maybe he likes you,' I said, but I didn't look at her, I didn't want to see it in her eyes. We couldn't look each other in the eye. She embraced me. 'I have you and the children. You're my man.' She held me close and we made love. That was the night before. For days, months, and years, I've gone over every gesture from that night, turning every caress into a blow to the head, the skin . . . until my hands are covered in blood. Love turns into hatred."

"What was he like, the American?"

"A man. He knew how to do things, he came from far away. He wanted a real woman, I can understand that. He wasn't the point. It was about her."

Like Luna. Maybe she has someone now, but not when she left.

WE HAVE TO cross the stream. If I don't help her, she'll slip and hurt herself.

"Give me your hand, and put your feet exactly where I put mine."

"I can do it by myself."

"No you can't."

Give him your hand, Marina, or you'll fall. Your legs are trembling.

She's all sweaty and red in the face. She's exhausted but won't admit it.

Her small hand is covered in sweat. She has nice nails. She turns around and I see her face. Red. Exhausted.

"I'd like to stop and wash my face."

"The cows do their business in that water. You'd better not."

"At least my hands. I'm sweating."

"Let's get to the other side, then we can stop."

Why did I follow him? There's no one around. Marco is asleep, and I'm exhausted.

"Are we far?"

Finally.

"Don't talk. You must be careful here."

He squeezes my hand with his hard muscles, and it hurts. The water forms little eddies. The noise is deafening but the baby doesn't wake up. I can see his boots in front of me. I can't keep going.

"Can I wash my hands now?"

"Yes, but don't drink."

She runs her wet hand through the sweaty curls against her neck. Then she looks straight into my eyes.

"I'm tired. Are we far?"

"We still have to reach the moraine, past the forest. There's a table there, and we can eat."

"We've walked almost an hour, we must be close. Didn't you say this was a shortcut?"

"We were walking slowly."

"It didn't seem like it."

"If it's too hard for you, I can slow down."

You can't get me, you bastard. I'm stronger than you.

"No, I'm fine."

She's stubborn. She doesn't give up.

"Let's go then."

9

HE BITES INTO the bread and cheese and says, without looking at me, "You can let him roam around, there's no danger here."

"What about the rocks? He could fall and hurt himself."

"He'll learn; there's nothing to be afraid of."

It's quiet here among the rocks, with no one around. Just the three of us, the table, two benches, and the crucifix overhead, planted in the ground. Red droplets descend from the crown of thorns on his forehead, his eyes are half closed, and his body is covered with wounds. Marco plays with two rocks and stares at the crucifix. I search for a topic of conversation.

"These crucifixes are so realistic, children find them scary."

"The stuff on TV is worse."

"Maybe, but Marco doesn't watch TV yet."

"They see so much."

He said there's no danger here. I wonder what he meant. He's staring at me. What does he want from me?

"Do you work in the city?"

"Yes, I'll go back to work at the end of the summer."

"What do you do?"

"I work in a company, I do the books."

"Do you enjoy it?"

"Yes."

"More than being a mother?"

"Don't put words in my mouth! They're two different things. One is my job and the other is my life. Do you like being a guide?"

"It's my life. I've been climbing the mountain since I was a kid."

"Did you like being a father?"

"I still am. I'm separated from the mother, not from Simon and Clara."

"Well, then, do you like being a father?"

"I do. They don't always like to be my kids. They don't like to get up early, they don't want to go up the mountain. We always used to argue with my wife about it."

"Is your wife less strict than you are?"

"Maybe. When they were little, we saw things the same way, but then she changed."

"When children come into the picture it's more difficult to see eye to eye."

"Did that happen to you?"

"No . . . A little. You feel alone, your husband works, and when he comes home, you're tired. You begin to have two lives. But maybe it's just me."

What did I just say? I'm crazy! What possessed me to say such a thing?

"What do you mean 'it's just you'?"

"I just meant that at first it's a bit difficult."

He stares at me. What a fool I am to say such a thing. Marco walks over to him and touches the ice axe. The man speaks brusquely, as he had earlier in the cable car: "Don't touch. Come here."

He picks him up and ties his shoelaces. Now he touches the stitches. Marco pulls his head away.

"How many stitches?"

"Six."

He puts the boy down and gives him a piece of bread. Marco stands next to him, with his hand on the man's leg. Say something, Marina. Don't give him time to ask any more questions.

"Why is it called the Rifugio della Dama?"

"It's a local legend. A long time ago, a woman and her guide died there. There's a pile of rocks at the top. Whoever gets there leaves a stone for good luck."

"How did she die?"

"I don't know. Perhaps it isn't even true. Tourists like stories, mountain tragedies. The papers are full of them. If a guide dies, it's a big to-do. My father used to tell us that the Dama was the Snow Queen, who lived beneath the ice, and she would come out to keep lonely men company. The glacier melts away completely now, so no more Snow Queen. No one to keep lonely men company."

"Perhaps they're better off, as you say."

She has a sense of humor, this one. "At least they know what they're dealing with. Women are strange."

I laugh. "I'd never heard that one. Funny!"

Let's see if she keeps laughing. "They're dangerous."

"Really!"

"They strike when you're not looking. There's not much to laugh about, is there, Marco?"

A pause.

"Why did you say that to the child?"

"He'll be a man one day and he has to begin to understand women, to know that they're not to be trusted."

I can barely swallow. I can't breathe. All around us there are boulders, piled on top of each other, frozen in place, with a crucifix on top. Like the Via Crucis. Why did I come here? My voice is hoarse. "Do you really have such little esteem for women?"

"One feels esteem for a friend, someone who deserves it."

"Are you saying that men and women can't be friends?"

"No, they can't. Let's go."

He stands up, puts away the bag of sandwiches, picks up Marco, puts him in his backback, and loads it on his back. The baby doesn't make a sound. He turns toward me and repeats, in the same voice, "Let's go."

The bumpkin laughs. His face wrinkles up. He has the eyes of a naughty child. Marco laughs with him, at me.

I look for something to say. "I'll put a sweater on him. He may get cold."

The man doesn't answer. I feel pathetic. My legs hurt. The two of them are already far ahead of me, trudging through the rocks, happy and carefree.

WE'VE LEFT HER behind. I talk to the boy so he won't be scared without his mother.

"When my brothers and I were young, we used to run through these rocks, and the first one home ate everyone's lunch. Are you still hungry, Marco?"

"Yes."

"At the lodge, you'll have a nice plate of pasta. Mamma gives you mush, but you want spaghetti."

I see her out of the corner of my eye. She's struggling far behind. I hear her call out, but pretend not to. I'll pick up the pace and we'll leave her here on the mountain. Let's see if she can make it on her own.

"Does your head still hurt, Marco?"

"Yes."

"You understand everything I say, don't you? Your mother did that to you. Now you know and she won't trick you again."

He turns back and gazes at her. When we're little, we understand things without the need for words.

"Mamma coming?"

"She's coming. We'll walk ahead and she'll join us later."

It's all useless. No matter what your mother does to you, you still long for her. Mamma coming?

"I don't know how this will end, Marco, but your mother has to confess. She has to tell the truth. She'll cry, pull her hair, and then she'll be forced to say what she did. After that, we'll wait for your father and tell him everything."

"Daddy."

"Yes, Daddy. Who knows what he's like. Maybe he won't care, or maybe he won't believe us. She tells him what he wants to hear, and he's easily convinced. It takes guts to stand up to your wife and to keep your child safe. That's why she has to tell the truth, to us and to him. We're not stupid. Even if sometimes we pretend to be. You know that, don't you Marco? It can be useful to play dumb, so they leave us alone. But if we want the truth, we can get it. We're strong. You can do without her, Marco, just imagine she never existed. She did her job, she brought you into the world, and now we'll get rid of her.

"Mamma coming?"

"Stop that."

"Mamma coming?"

"I said don't cry! Stop that! Or why not, go ahead and cry. It will pass."

BASTARD! WHERE IS he going with my baby?

I won't lose you! I won't get lost, and I won't slow down, even if I can't feel my legs and my blisters are burning, and tears are flowing down my face. I can see them, far ahead. The bastard is speeding up; now he's disappearing behind a pile of rocks. Don't be afraid, Marina, don't give up. I'll call out to them.

"Marco! Marco!"

Don't scream, stay strong, focus. Don't lose your head. He's your baby, and that man has no proof, the police didn't believe him. He thinks he can blackmail me. There are signs along the trail, follow them. Keep going, don't cry, think.

It will take time, but you'll get there and you'll turn him in to the police. The sun is shining, just follow the markings.

You were strong as a girl, when did you get so weak? How could you do what you did? It doesn't matter, don't think about it, it never happened. I must be stronger than he is; otherwise he'll have me in the palm of his hand. He hates women, he's a psychopath. I call out: "Marco, Marco!"

He won't hurt the boy. I am the enemy in his eyes. I collapse onto a boulder. I can see the whole scene in my head.

Marco is crying, he won't stop. He has blood on his head. I slip, and now we're both on the ground, amid shards of glass, oil, and wine. I can't get up, I don't have the strength. Trapped in my own dark tunnel, suddenly I go blank, blind, and I hit his head against the table. I did it. His mother.

There are rocks everywhere, and dust. The sky is icy and pale. There's no one around. Can't I fix what I've done? Can I go back in time?

LOOKING OVER PHOTOS in the album, it all seems easy. For his second birthday, I baked a cake, and the house was full of children. A big success.

At night he would wake up, sometimes every hour. I sat on the floor next to his bed. My back hurt, I was sleepy, and I sang to him. I couldn't bring him into the big bed with me, it's not allowed. I would take him to the park in the morning, and then again in the afternoon so he could tire himself out. This was our world. Two more carousel rides, only two, or we'll be late. Don't put rocks in your mouth. What am I doing wrong? What was my mistake?

I tried to plan ahead for all the potential problems so I wouldn't be taken by surprise, but it didn't work. I was too distracted, just like when I was a little girl.

"Marina, what are you dreaming about? Where are you?"

"I'm here, Mamma."

I must organize my thoughts, concentrate, prepare: do the groceries, cook, sleep, come home, go to the park, organize parties, take care of him when he has the flu, call the doctor. Then there's Mario, my mother, my sisters, happiness, judgment.

ONE DAY WE came back from the park with the stroller— just like every other day—with the groceries. Called the elevator, looked for the keys. Where are the keys? I've locked myself out again.

I sat on the floor of the elevator—like I am sitting today on these rocks—and cried. This is all women are good for. I've heard it time and again. The baby stared at me and grabbed a package of cookies from the grocery bag. He bit into it; he was hungry. I knew exactly what Mario would say.

"Again! Go to your mother's and wait for me there."

And my mother: "Locked out, again? Marina, where is your head?"

They'll never know; I refuse to tell them.

The baby started to cry.

"Let go of those cookies!"

We got out of the elevator with our groceries. The baby was crying. We went to the locksmith.

"I want you to open this goddamned door with a credit card, like a thief."

He came with me, opened the door, and finally I was inside, safe. Mario would never know.

The locksmith stared at me with compassion. I could fall in love with a man like that, a plumber, an electrician, a builder, a locksmith, a mechanic. Before making love he would fix the door, the washing machine, the car motor.

It was late. The baby was asleep in the stroller, with the bag of cookies still in his hands, unopened. I could have let him eat a few cookies before lunch, but it's not allowed because it spoils his appetite. Now it was too late to eat. Too late for everything.

GET UP. WALK. Catch up. He ran off with your baby.

I see a bird in the sky, flying above the mountaintops. Is it an eagle? It never stops. I wonder what it sees from the icy heights? A landscape of rocks, mountain peaks. A woman sitting on a boulder.

Why am I crying? The baby is with him. You're free. Go back to the town, pick up a few things, and leave. Flag down a car on the road.

Stop at a hotel and sleep for two days. When you wake up, decide where to go, and with whom. Confess: "I give up. I'm not up to it. I don't know how to be a mother."

Mario can take care of the baby. During the day he could leave him with my mother and then pick him up in the evenings. My sisters would take him to the seaside. I could live anywhere, in a little house, with a job, money of my own. I would go to the movies and on long walks and I could have a man if I wanted, or live by myself, in peace and quiet. Like this spot. I could let my thoughts wander, daydream. Stories, loves, parties . . . And no one would get hurt.

At night, if I missed him, I could look at a photo, the one where he's wearing a red sweater. I would look at the photo and talk to him.

It would be better for everyone. Papà would read you stories. Grandma would help out, and your aunties too. You wouldn't want for anything. And I wouldn't be able to hurt you. It's right that I should only have a photograph.

"ARE YOU FEELING all right?"

Who are these people? I didn't see them arrive. A man and a woman. The Austrians from the gondola. No, Italians. A young girl stands silently to one side, watching me.

"I need to catch up with my son and the guide. I stopped to rest and now I don't know the way."

"Were they headed toward the lodge?"

"Yes."

"We're going that way. Come with us."

I stand up and look at the sky. The eagle is gone. The sky is empty.

10

THE LODGE IS a two-story building made of stone and wood. This is the place from which his mother fled. There are flowers in the windows, and billowing curtains. In the winter it must be covered in fog. Like a mirage; it looks close, but then you walk and walk and you never get there. Now I feel like I could keep going for hours. I can't feel my legs or my feet.

He's not outside; maybe he's inside with Marco. During the climb I planned my revenge. I dried my tears. He'll never see me cry again. No more crying, yelling, complaining, making excuses. I must stand firm if I want to keep my baby.

On the way there, I talked to the couple and their young daughter.

"How old are you?"

"What class are you in?"

"You're a good walker."

"She's used to it—we've always taken her with us, even when she was little."

"How clever of you."

They asked me about Marco. I answered as if everything were perfectly normal.

"How far are we from the lodge?"

I'd like to ask after every turn, but I don't. I grin and bear it; I'm strong, and the hatred I feel sustains me. I'll confront him, and I won't let him blackmail me.

When I was young I knew how to be cruel, and no one got the better of me. When the baby was born, I forgot how to be cruel. If you can't be cruel when you need to, you become cruel for real. We came to a stop in front of the lodge.

"Here we are."

"Are you going in?"

"We're heading up to the lake. We brought sandwiches."

I go up three stone steps. I stop in front of a window on the porch to check my reflection. I'm flushed, my hair is a mess; I look terrible. I fix my hair, take a handkerchief out of my bag, and wipe off the sweat. I have lipstick with me; I apply a thin layer to my lips. He'll be in shock.

I used to check my reflection in the shop windows on my way to school. I was never sure if I looked quite right, not too showy but not too dull.

I open the door and think of his mother's hand on that same door, the night she left. I imagine that I am his mother, come back to face my sons and husband.

Jackets hang from hooks in the hall. A stuffed woodchuck stands on its hind legs, staring at nothing, next to an old wooden sled. I hear a joyful clamor coming from the dining room. I stand in the doorway but I can't see them. There are people eating and talking at the tables. Behind the counter, two women serve drinks. Glassy-eyed elk and deer heads line the stone walls. He's at the last table, near the window, between another man and Marco. My baby has a napkin tied around his neck and he's eating spaghetti with his hands. His face is red with sauce. He has already forgotten me.

"THERE SHE IS. She made it."

"What did you expect, Manfred?"

Look at her, she's smiling. She's lost her marbles.

"What are you going to do, Manfred?"

"She has to confess, Albert, in front of a witness."

"It's none of your business. Why do you want to get mixed up in this? Who's going to believe you?"

"That's why she has to confess."

She walks calmly among the tables. She has even put on some makeup. People stare. What does she want? She leans over to kiss the baby.

"Hello, darling, how are you? Poor thing, you were hungry!"

Smile, Marina. Look friendly. "Thank you for carrying him all that way. He was ravenous, and I was so slow! I'm completely out of shape."

Smile at the man next to him as well. Hold out your hand. Everything must look normal, a meeting between civilized people.

"Hello, I'm Marina, Marco's mother."

"Albert, Manfred's brother."

The other brother, the one who owns the lodge. I'll bet he didn't have the guts to say anything.

She sits down as if nothing has happened, picks up the boy, and begins to feed him. Talk, talk.

"I exercise, but I wasn't prepared for the climb. By the way, I ran into two hikers, and they told me that it wasn't a shortcut at all! In fact, they said it's five kilometers longer that way. I guess your brother was trying to put me to the test. Now I feel strong, and it was such a pleasant hike! The mountain was so beautiful under the sun."

She kisses the boy and cleans his face.

"Was it good?"

She's crazy.

"He cried a little, but then he stopped."

"When he didn't see me, of course he cried. Maybe I should have waved, to let him know you were going away. But I didn't have the time. You disappeared so quickly."

They're listening. Don't stop now.

"Children have no sense of time. If their mother disappears for an hour, to them it's as if she'd left forever. They think she won't come back, that they've been abandoned. There's nothing more terrifying."

The brother is staring at me with interest.

"Did you study child psychology?"

Psychology! Albert has lost his mind. I just told him what she did to her son.

"No, but when I was pregnant with Marco I read a lot of books. I wanted to be ready to be a mother. It's the same for men too. Do you have children?"

"Yes, three. Two boys and a girl."

"Do they live here at the lodge?"

"Yes."

"They must not have many friends to play with up here."

"They don't really need them. When they go to school they play among themselves. We grew up the same way."

"Do you have good memories?"

"We were free, and we could go wherever we liked."

What is she aiming at? And Albert keeps answering her questions.

You thought you'd defeated me, you bastard, but you don't know me. Marco holds his fork out to me and offers me some cold spaghetti.

"Thank you, my darling, but I'm not hungry."

Keep talking to the brother, Marina, just act like he doesn't exist.

"You're right. They're free here, and the air is clean, and it's quiet."

I'll make you shut up, you foolish woman.

"Exactly. The dangers lie in the city, in people's homes."

Don't look at him, don't answer. Just ignore him.

"Manfred helped me when Marco hurt his head. He must have told you. He drove us to the hospital and took care of us. I was in such a terrible state! I couldn't remember anything and I could barely speak. I must not have made a very good impression! I was so afraid that he was badly hurt! I'm so grateful for his help. And now he's brought us here. It's a beautiful spot. Isolated but beautiful. I wonder if I could live in a place like this. Does your wife enjoy living here?"

"She's used to it."

"Is she one of the two women behind the bar?"

"Yes, the one with the dark hair."

"Excuse me, I need to change Marco. He's wet. Where can I take him?"

"The bathroom is downstairs. Take the stairs by the door."

I pick up the boy and squeeze him in my arms as I walk between the tables. My boy.

"MANFRED, DO YOU want to send away every woman you meet? You should see a doctor."

"She's just playing the role of the good mother for your benefit. That's all she does all day long. Albert, listen to me: I came into the kitchen, the baby was on the floor, out cold, lying in broken glass, with blood on his head. And she was hiding."

"She was terrified, like she said."

"Just think for a moment: the baby cried, she screamed, then there was a bang, and then nothing."

"Something similar happened to Bianca."

"What?"

"Silvia cries all the time, as you know. She's the youngest, the only girl, and we spoil her. One day Bianca spanked her and she started to cry. She wouldn't stop. She ran away, crying, slipped, and banged her head. I found Bianca sitting on a chair staring at her. Blood was pouring out of the child's head."

"And what if you'd been outside, banging on the door like crazy? Wouldn't Bianca have opened the door?"

"Manfred, forget about it. That woman has read all sorts of books, she knows more than you or I. You haven't gotten over what happened with Luna."

"Explain this to me: I walk off with her baby and leave her on the mountain by herself and she yells at us to wait for her. But now she strolls in, perfectly calm. Even thanks me for carrying him up here and feeding him. 'So kind of you,' she says."

"So?"

"She has something to hide. If someone did that with one of my children, I'd punch him."

"Because you're crazy, Manfred. That's why Luna left you."

"YOU'RE ALL WET, even your pants! But your cheeks are nice and pink."

"Pink."

"Yes, pink! Were you scared without your mamma?"

He stares at me in silence. What are they thinking when they do that? Will he forget that night, in the kitchen?

"Hold still, I'm almost done."

The door opens and I turn around. The brown-haired woman from the bar, the brother's wife, is standing there.

"You can come over to our place. It's not very comfortable in here, or clean."

"Thank you, I'm almost done."

"No, please, come."

"All right, thank you then. I have to change him completely; his pants are wet. You're Manfred's brother's wife, aren't you?"

"Bianca, Albert's wife."

We go up the stairs. I follow her. On the second floor I glance down the dark, narrow hallway.

"These are the guest rooms. Our apartment is upstairs."

She opens a door like the others, and we step into their apartment. It's clean, with lots of blond wood.

"How lovely it is here."

"We just redid the apartment. The rest of the lodge is old and has never been renovated. It's expensive. You can change him there."

"Thank you."

The house is pleasant. There are three beds, and lots of toys. They sleep together, as I did with my sisters. I'd like to lie down and be protected by this kind woman. I don't want to be alone with Marco anymore.

"Albert said to tell you . . ."

I look up at her.

"That he apologizes on his brother's behalf."

"Manfred?"

"Yes. For taking the boy, bringing him up here, and leaving you along the way. He has crazy ideas. He's not really crazy; it's just that his wife left him and took the kids. Manfred suffered a lot. He's angry with women, all of them."

"I noticed."

We laugh.

"When he comes up here, he barely says hello to me and just asks where his brother is. I'd like to hear about his kids, Simon and Clara. They grew up here, and I care for them. Luna used to bring them up here to play with our kids, and we miss them. Luna and I were friends. The Sanes are all quiet types, but Manfred is a real bear. Let me get you a clean towel."

She leaves the room.

I don't have to avenge myself. This time it's he who took a false step. He could have blackmailed me and forced me to talk, and maybe I would have succumbed. But he didn't have the courage to confront me. No one believes him. He's crazy and he hates women.

Bianca hands me a towel.

"You can hang his pants to dry on the balcony."

"Thank you."

The bathroom is neat, the kitchen is all wood, and there are geraniums on the balcony. I don't want to go back to the apartment in town, with Manfred downstairs. I'm afraid of the kitchen now. I can see the broken bottles on the floor, oil and wine everywhere, the baby with his eyes closed, blood. I can still smell the wine.

"It's so nice here. If I hadn't rented the place in town I would stay awhile."

"There are a few empty rooms."

"But I've already paid for the apartment."

"As you wish. Do you want to eat?"

"No, he already ate. I'll put him down for a nap outside on the grass; he's tired. Thank you for everything. If you don't mind I'll come get his pants later."

"See you later."

MAYBE I'M WRONG about her, and Albert is right.

"You need a woman, Manfred. You spend too much time alone."

Who needs a woman? I've been through hell; I've earned my solitude.

I go out on the terrace. There she is, lying on the grass. The baby is asleep on top of her, and she has her eyes closed.

Deep down, I hate this place, but I keep coming back. With my clients, and to see Albert. We used to spend hours on that swing; now his kids play there. I have a memory of her, hanging laundry near the swing, just as Bianca does now. Nothing changes.

How can Albert stand to live here and see them do the same things we did? She wakes them in the morning, bathes them, dresses them for school, kisses them before they leave the house. Just like when we were kids.

IN THE AFTERNOONS, when we came home, our mother would give us hot tea and three slices of the cake she had made for the guests. She set them aside for us.

"You're freezing! How was school today?"

Then she would send us off to play.

"Manfred, you go too! Stop hanging around, I need to cook!"

That day when we came home from school, she wasn't there. The cleaning lady had left us two slices of bread each and a cube of butter. We had to spread it ourselves. The butter was cold, and the bread crumbled under the knife.

They too have three children; it's just like it was, at least until the day Bianca decides she's had enough. Some people are like that; they repeat the same things. Others do the opposite; they try to sever all links to the past.

THEY'RE ASLEEP TOGETHER, on the grass. Albert told me I should apologize, but I won't do it. I'm not convinced that things happened as she says. I trust Albert, but I trust myself more. I look up at the summit of the Gigante. Mountains don't change either.

BEFORE FALLING ASLEEP, I look out at the summit of the Gigante from my first-floor window. I'm sure that the giant is asleep in his mountain lair, with boulders and trees piled on top of him. If he should wake and emerge from his lair, the earth would tremble and the lodge would be swallowed up.

Children think more than we do.

Ever since Simon and Clara went away, I walk in order to keep myself from thinking and to forget the pain in my stomach. I went to the doctor once.

"There's nothing wrong with you, Manfred. I'll give you some drops to calm your nerves."

I didn't buy them.

I didn't mean to hit her. And anyway, that's not why she left. I didn't mean to do it. The hatred was inside of me. I didn't mean to bang her against the wall and make her nose bleed. She fell to the ground. She stared at me in silence; she couldn't believe it. I couldn't either. I didn't mean to hit her in the face; I wanted to hit myself, to rid myself of her.

It's three o'clock, time to go. I'll see if she wants to take the jeep into town, if she's tired. But I won't apologize.

I STAND OVER them as they lie in the meadow, blocking their sun. She opens her eyes.

"It's three o'clock, we should be getting back."

She starts.

"You startled me."

The bumpkin smiles. His face creases, and he looks like an old man. Marco stands up, ready to follow him, but I hold him tight.

"Go ahead, don't wait for us."

He stares at me, confused. "Are you going down on your own?"

"Yes, later. Or maybe we'll stay up here."

He's stunned. "You'll stay here?"

"Yes, maybe. They told me there's a fair this Sunday, the Festa della Dama, in honor of the woman who died on the mountain with her guide. There will be dancing, a venison roast, it sounds like fun.

"I know. I was born here."

"Yes, of course."

"But you didn't bring anything with you."

"I have what I need for three days. I'll manage. I have three diapers. And Bianca said she'll ask Albert to buy me some more tomorrow."

"Bianca will ask Albert?"

"Yes, your brother."

"Ah. So I shouldn't wait for you?"

"Marco, say good-bye to Manfred! Say bye-bye, thank you, and see you soon!"

"Bye-bye."

"Bravo, my darling."

"Well, good-bye then."

"Good-bye. This way you won't have to hear him cry for a few days."

He turns around. He didn't seem too happy; he wasn't expecting this.

HOW DID SHE manage to get the better of me? I don't understand. It's my fate: to feel stronger, and then lose. First Luna, and now this one.

"Wait!" she calls out.

"What?"

"The keys to the apartment. Tomorrow the carpenter is coming to repair the door. Could you leave the keys in the umbrella stand?"

11

I PEER AT MY watch. It's eight o'clock. Marco has slept
through the night. I run over to the crib. He's lying on his
stomach with his hands in fists, wrapped in Mario's old sweater.
I listen closely; he's breathing. I sit back down on the bed.
Maybe I've awoken into a different life? I'm not sleepy. I woke
up on my own, not startled by a baby's cry. It's the first time in
two years. I climb back under the covers and try to remember
my dream. It dissolves into the worn upholstery in the room,
the old stains, familiar landscapes. Framed in the window I can
see a single mountain, a little bit apart from the others. Enor-
mous boulders form the profile of a sleeping man. I've been told
that this is the Gigante.

This was the room where the three boys, abandoned by
their mother, once slept. When Albert and Bianca were married, they moved upstairs. The setting of their childhood lone-
liness is now one of ten hotel rooms. Bianca showed me around.

"This is where the boys slept, when the family lived on this floor."

Last night I discovered a secret drawing on the wall next to the bed. Between two faded flowers, there hid a tiny figure wearing glasses, standing on skis. None of the boys wears glasses. Who could it be? A friend? Their father?

I didn't tell Mario about my decision to stay here. Too complicated, and pointless. The floor boards are black. The lodge is old. I bathed Marco in the sink attached to the wall. In the afternoon, he played with Bianca's children.

"Don't worry, the two elder boys will take care of him. They're used to it. They look after their little sister."

They play behind the house. On the swing, on a pile of sand with little buckets and shovels, and amid the laundry hung out to dry. Under the woodshed, where a cat recently had her kittens. Every so often I check on him. Marco is drunk with glee; he holds a kitten in his arms, and lets himself be pushed on the swing by the eldest; he pours a pail of sand on the little one. In the evening, he falls asleep as I'm bathing him.

MANFRED APPEARED IN my dream, wearing glasses. I see his face, covered in wrinkles, and his light-colored eyes, the malicious smile, but he is the same size as Marco. I introduce him to Mario.

"He's our child. You don't know him. I'm sorry, but this is how he came out. We don't get to choose."

"I don't like him."

"Too bad. There's nothing we can do."

Then, we go outside to play in the garden. Now I'm Silvia, Bianca's little girl, and Manfred pushes me on the swing. We crawl under the woodshed to see the kittens. It's snowing. The kittens are gone, but there is blood on the snow. The cat sleeps. Manfred kicks her awake.

The dream was not upsetting. The swing, the snow, the woodshed, our games. Manfred's kick felt good, and so did seeing the traces of blood, not yet concealed by the snow.

Marco sits up and looks over at me.

"Good morning! You slept well! Let's get dressed and go down for some breakfast. Then we can go play with the kids. Does that sound nice?"

"Yes."

SHE SAID, "COULD you leave the keys for the carpenter?"

Next, she'll tell me to pack her things and bring them up to the lodge. I'll put the keys in the umbrella rack and leave.

It's gray out. Tourists are arriving for the feast; they've asked me to take them up to the lodge for the roast. The idea that she's up there with Bianca and Albert doesn't sit well. She'll ask questions, stick her nose into our business, and Bianca has never been on my side.

BIANCA AND LUNA were friends. She protected Luna, and they confided in each other. They would lower their voices whenever Albert or I came into the room. Albert didn't care.

"Who cares? We also talk about things that we don't want them to hear."

"What do we talk about?"

"About Caterina's ass, and how much we'd like to sleep with her."

"Exactly, nothing. You don't know women, Albert."

Once, I hid behind a door and listened to them.

"Albert has bad breath."

Luna answered right away: "Yes, it's the onion. Once, Manfred stayed in town. I ate in front of the TV and slept diagonally across the bed. I thought to myself—if he doesn't come back, I'll be sad, but I'll adapt."

And they laughed.

"Women don't need us, Albert."

"Don't be silly. We don't need them either. Look at our father."

But now that he's old he's found himself a woman. Maybe it's Caterina, the one with the nice ass. One day I'll show up unannounced and find out who it is.

Next time Simon and Clara come, I'll take some time off. I called them yesterday, but they don't talk. They just answer yes or no.

Luna doesn't say much either. I told her: "Put them on the train and I'll come get them. It's only an hour."

"They're still young, Manfred, they can't travel on their own."

"So come with them."

"I'm busy at school."

She doesn't want to see me.

I LOOK AT the broken door, mended with a board. I haven't been inside the apartment since that night. It's my house. I'll go in and look around, that's all. I turn the key and push.

It still smells of wine. The armoire in the bedroom is open. There are clothes on the chairs, and the beds are unmade.

There is a photo on the dresser. Three girls. I look more closely. They claim that nearsightedness improves with age. I should get new lenses. The eye inside sees clearly, but no one knows that.

She must be the one on the left, the only one with dark hair. How old is she? Eight, ten? And the others? They must be sisters, friends.

Next to the photograph there is a small notebook. It contains shopping lists, drawings of flowers, houses, mountains. Maybe she makes them for the boy.

I pick up the book on the dresser and a sheet of paper falls out. I open it and sit down on the unmade bed.

You've slept in Marco's room the last three nights. I don't know why, you won't tell me. You say, "If you don't understand, I can't explain it to you." I don't know what changed between us, please tell me. Now you're going away to the mountains and we still haven't talked about it. I wanted to go away with you for a few days, and your mother offered to keep Marco. You said that

you don't want to be away from him. You don't want to leave
him, but he drives you crazy and you cry. I'm worried about
you, about us. I send you all the kisses that you no longer want
to give me.

A letter from her husband. "I'm worried about you." Not
enough, it would seem . . .

The baby drives her crazy. Did you hear that, Albert? I'm
not mad; I'm the only one who knows the truth, even if I don't
have the proof and you say that I have it in for women.

I fold the letter and place it back in the notebook.

A rubber duck floats in soapy water in the bathtub. A drop
of water falls on his beak. I shut the faucet. Marco's toy boat is
at the other end, next to a tiger and a giraffe.

In the kitchen a dirty coffee cup sits on the table. I stop at
the spot where I saw the baby lying on the floor, on his side,
with his eyes closed. From the door I couldn't see that he had
blood on his head; he looked like he was sleeping, under the
table. How did he end up there? If he had fallen he wouldn't be
there. I sit down in front of the cup. There are coffee stains on
the wrinkled paper tablecloth, and crumbs.

She's alone. When she left him in the stroller in front of the
house, she said: "I was making his lunch."

She has to do everything while the baby is sleeping. That
day, when it rained, they didn't go out; it was almost dark. A
long day. It used to be that way with Luna as well.

She would climb into bed, exhausted.

"I don't know what to do with them when it rains. Good
thing you came home, Manfred."

Good thing I was here that night, too. I've been thinking about it for a few days. I get down on all fours under the table. There are long red stains, streaks—is it wine or oil? I grab a corner of the paper tablecloth, moisten it with saliva, and rub. Then I sniff the stain. It's not wine.

She didn't even bother to wash the blood. I put the tablecloth in my pocket.

"YOU HAVE TO let the venison hang for one or two days."

"Poor thing. Such a beautiful animal."

"There are lots of them in the mountains. Have you ever tasted venison?"

Bianca immerses the meat in oil and vinegar. Sara, the girl who helps out in the kitchen, chops garlic and onion. The kitchen is hot; there are pots and pans on the walls and the stove in the middle, a brick oven in one corner. It's raining outside. The two boys are in town with their father, doing the shopping. Marco is eating at the kitchen table with Silvia; he takes pieces of steak in his hands and shoves them into his mouth. Yesterday he spit out his mush; he wants to eat the same things as the big kids now.

"Take smaller bites."

He doesn't listen, just watches Silvia and imitates her.

"I like your kitchen. It's nice and big."

"I'd like to have it redone. It's old, almost the same as when I arrived. I repainted it and bought new pots and dishes. Everything was chipped, and the pans were all black. No one ever bought anything new. My father-in-law refused. He would say,

It's a mountain lodge, not a fancy hotel. And I would tell him that these days, people want to eat well and be comfortable, even in a lodge. When he left, I bought everything new. But we should have it redone."

"Did he go live in the valley?"

"No, he went to the city. He changed his life completely. I can understand why."

Sara looks over at us.

"How did he manage, with three kids and the lodge to run?"

"Two women came to clean and cook. The three boys helped out after school. They would chop wood, shovel snow, serve tables in the restaurant."

"A tough childhood."

"The work wasn't so bad. I used to help my mother in town. The first time I spoke to Albert he was fourteen and I was twelve. After school they would take the bus and then the gondola, and their father would come pick them up in the snowcat. He never saw anyone. I had a crush on Albert. I would watch him and smile. I knew that it wasn't a good idea to try to talk to the Sane brothers, that they easily lost their tempers; usually they didn't answer at all. They only talked when they had to, when the teacher asked them a question. I don't know how I got up the courage."

Sara begins to laugh. "Everyone around here knows what happened next, even our kids."

Silvia smiles and looks over at her mother. She likes to hear the story of how her parents met.

"One day after school, I went over to him. Quickly, without

thinking, I said, 'If you want, my mother can make you a cake for your birthday.' Everyone used to bring a cake on their birthday, except for them."

"What did he say?"

"'I don't want your stupid cake.'"

Sara and Silvia laugh. Marco laughs too, without knowing why.

"What did you do?"

"I started to cry, as if he'd hit me. I cried and I stood there. I couldn't believe he had said that: I don't want your stupid cake. But he didn't leave either, that was the thing. He was terrified by my tears. Manfred and Stefan pulled him away. After that day, from time to time he would talk to me, if his brothers weren't around."

Sara stood there, knife in hand, her eyes red from the onions, or so she claimed.

"You were brave to marry Albert."

Bianca laughs and dips a piece of venison in the oil.

"Never trust the nice ones. They make life seem like a fairy tale, and we all know how that ends."

Silvia gets up; she wants to play. Marco follows her.

"Marco, you haven't finished eating. Silvia will wait for you, isn't that right?"

The little girl nods, sits down again. Her brothers have raised her well.

"Mamma will help, that way you'll finish more quickly."

Bianca points to the wound on his head. "Quite a bump."

I nod, without looking at her.

"How many stitches?"

Answer calmly, don't get upset. "Six. His hair is starting to grow back. By the time his father comes, it will be almost gone."

"Daddy's coming."

I hug him. "Yes, Daddy's coming, good boy."

Bianca stops working and looks over at us. "When is he coming?"

"In ten days. We're going to the beach. My mother and sisters are already there."

"His father doesn't know that he hurt himself?"

"Yes, of course, but I'd rather he didn't see the scar. Or my mother either, for that matter. Luckily it's behind the hairline. Come on, Marco, take one more bite and then you can go play."

Bianca cleans her daughter's face.

"Go play in your room; you're a nuisance downstairs in the hall. Take care of the baby, now."

"Can we go outside?"

"Can't you see it's raining?"

"When will Christian and Gabriel be back?"

"In a little while; there was a lot of shopping to do. Go play with Marco."

Silvia takes his hand and sighs.

I reassure her: "Don't worry, I'll be there in fifteen minutes so he can take his nap."

They leave the room, hand in hand. Maybe I should have another child.

"It must be easier to raise children when you have more than one."

"Yes, but it was hard at first. The two boys were born only eleven months apart."

"Eleven months! That must have been terrible."

"Later it was easier. They played together, and when Silvia was born, they helped me with her."

"You've done a good job."

"Marrying Albert or raising my children?"

"Everything: raising your children, managing the lodge."

"There are days when I can't stand being up here, not having a moment to myself. Sometimes, I'd like to just get up and go."

We stare at her.

"I know everyone asks, Will Bianca be able to stand it? But if I left, I wouldn't be able to stop thinking about them. Albert even more than the children. I think for the first ten years he almost expected me to leave; he practically willed it to happen. 'It will happen to me, just like it happened to my father.' Now I think he's resigned to the idea that I'm going to stay."

"It happened to Manfred."

"Yes, he managed to push Luna away. Since she left with the kids, he seems calmer. He used to be nervous all the time, and he had attacks of rage. He never slept, and he would take it out on her and the children. He couldn't get used to it."

"Attacks of rage?"

Bianca goes quiet. She feels guilty for having spoken, and thinks of her husband.

"He never hurt them, of course, but once in a while he would spend the night at Stefan's, to cool down. He should never have married, that's the truth."

"Were you and Luna friends?"

"Yes. I miss her."

IT'S MORE HUMID in the city than in the mountains. It gets into your bones. The cars spray water when you cross the street and people's umbrellas drip on your shoulders. By seven thirty, my father has already eaten and washed the dishes. That way he won't ask me to stay for dinner; he's a terrible cook. I'll have a beer with him, and then I'll go out for a pizza. Just to see how he's doing. I haven't seen him in two weeks. He calls me on Sundays.

"How are you?"

"Fine. How are you?"

"Fine."

When I visit I don't stay long. We never know what to say; sometimes we talk about the lodge. He's afraid to ask Albert.

"If I ask he gets offended. He thinks I'm keeping tabs."

I tell him about the tourists, the house, Albert's three kids. He wants to hear about my children as well. Maybe this time his girlfriend will be there. Maybe he'll marry her. He's free to do it. After all, he already divided everything between his sons, he has nothing left. He's a clever one. I ring the bell. The building where he lives is modern, depressing; the windows have no balconies.

"Who is it?"

"Manfred."

The stairwells are dark. I never take the elevator. Here he is, at the door. Already in his pajamas at eight o'clock.

"Hello, Manfred."

"Hello, Dad."

"Why don't you call before coming over?"

He closes the door. Jackets and hats hang on hooks by the door, as they did up at the lodge. They were the first thing we saw when we came home from school.

"Do you have visitors?" I look toward the living room.

"Yes, of course."

The television is on.

"I'll turn it off, don't worry."

I sit on the couch; he sits on the armchair. He shuts off the game show with the remote control.

"Do they win money?"

"Sometimes."

"Do you enjoy it?"

"What?"

"Television."

"Not really. It keeps me company."

"Could I have a beer?"

"Yes, just a minute."

The furniture is all new. The carpet was a gift from us: Luna and me. We left the kids with Bianca and spent two days in the city on our own.

LUNA WAS EXCITED, she wanted to walk around the city. Suddenly she hugged me. Her eyes were shining. She wanted to buy clothes and toys. I waited outside. I couldn't tell her how I felt. I didn't even understand it myself. Rage toward her happiness. She came out of a shop and gave me a kiss.

"What's wrong?"

"Nothing."

My silence drove her crazy.

She stopped in front of a shop window with a display of carpets.

"Let's buy one for your father. His house is so cold."

"He doesn't want a carpet."

"He's different now that he lives in the city."

"Different how?"

She smiled at me; she was even more beautiful now than when we had met, more mature, maternal, secure. Why did I feel such hatred?

"He's sweeter. At Christmas he even gave me a kiss."

THIS NEW MAN comes into the room with a beer.

"Here you go, it's nice and cold."

"Thank you."

He sits down and looks at me.

"It's raining. Let's hope August is sunny. Otherwise there won't be many tourists. How is Stefan doing?"

"He wants to start selling sports gear, not only rent it. He went to talk to a supplier."

"That takes money. And then if it doesn't sell, you're stuck with the stuff. But it's his business now. How about Albert?" He still cares about the lodge.

"They have a good amount of guests for July. The lodge is almost full."

She's there now. I kept the bloody tablecloth. This time I'll get her.

"How about the kids? And Bianca?"

"Fine. I don't talk to them much."

"And your kids?"

"I talked to them yesterday."

"You should keep them with you longer, especially Simon. The little one is still young, and Luna is good with them."

I feel the rage flame up like a fire under my skin. "She's good with them?"

"She took them, she was wrong to do that, but she was a good wife, Manfred."

"Like yours."

In all those years, I had never mentioned it. Not even as a kid or as a young man. I never asked him about his wife, or wanted to see her shadow in his eyes. I was still satisfied with the story about the Snow Queen that he used to tell us in the snowcat.

He smiles. "I'm glad to hear you talk about it. You've never done it before. I've talked about it with your brothers."

"I'm happy for you, but I don't care."

He sits quietly, staring at his hands. I take one last sip of beer. I'm about to leave.

"You were the most attached to her. She protected you, and it made me furious. You had that problem with your eyes, and she didn't want you to suffer."

I get up and leave the beer glass on the table. "I'm going. It's late. Albert wants to take you to the town fair. Do you want to come?"

"Are you going?"

"I'm taking some tourists."

"We'll see."

"Good night."

"Good night, Manfred."

I RUN MY finger over the drawing on the wall: a small figure wearing glasses. It's hidden between two flowers in the wallpaper; you can only see it if you're lying in bed close to the wall. One eye, the left one, rolls inward and he has three hairs standing up on top of his head. The ski poles are like two little wings on either side of his body, and he is wearing short skis. His mouth is open, a perfect little black circle. Is he screaming? I can't tell.

One of the three boys drew the figure on the wall, one night when he couldn't sleep or some afternoon instead of doing his homework.

The mouth is open but there's no sound, like Marco when he suddenly stops crying. The sound stops, and then the light. I put my head under the pillow. The drawing reminds me of Marco when he's angry. One day I'll think about it, but not tonight. Tonight I'm happy. Another night. Why does this happen to me and not to other women? What do they have that I don't have? Patience, love, stoicism?

He falls asleep quickly, a minute after I put him to bed. He doesn't need a song or a story. He's happy here, maybe because everything is new and we're not alone. He gazes at Christian and Gabriel as if they were two heroes, and follows them around everywhere. Gabriel, the younger one, picks him up in his arms and carries him on his bicycle.

"Hold on tight!"

Marco puts his arms around Gabriel's waist, his face pressed against the boy's back. He laughs when Gabriel goes fast. I'm afraid he'll fall but I don't intervene because he's having too much fun. Gabriel likes to talk; he's like Bianca.

"I want a little brother like him, not a girl like Silvia."

Silvia shrugs, without looking at him.

"It's nice to have a sister. When you're older, she'll help you."

He doesn't believe me.

"She plays with dolls. She likes to play with Clara, but Clara went away."

"Is Clara Manfred's daughter?"

"Yes. She lives in the city, but a different one from where my grandfather lives."

Silvia interrupts. "She's coming soon."

"Are you happy?"

She nods. Then she reflects: "But Manfred doesn't bring her here."

"Why not?"

Gabriel answers first: "Yes he does, but just not every day or else she'll get spoiled."

I laugh. "Who spoils her?"

Silvia smiles. "Mamma."

Gabriel scolds her. "What are you saying?"

Silvia speaks quickly, so she won't be interrupted. "She gives her whatever she wants, cake and candy, and she lets her play with grown-up clothes. At night we talk in bed. But then when she goes home she whines and Manfred gets mad."

Gabriel laughs. "They put on my mother's shoes."

"Shut up, idiot!"

Marco watches them argue and laughs.

The older brother, Christian, is more like his father: he doesn't talk much.

This morning I ran into Albert. He smiled at me. "How is it going?"

"Very well."

"How is the boy?"

"He loves playing with your kids."

"I'm glad to hear it."

He doesn't speak any more than Manfred does, but the tone is friendlier. I can imagine the little girl who wanted to bring him a cake, and his reaction: I don't want your stupid cake.

TONIGHT BIANCA SAT next to me. The children were running around frantically before going to bed. She was drinking a tisane.

"Are you tired?"

"We're almost full, and more people are coming for the fair."

"Do you need the room?"

"No, we're fine. Tomorrow another girl will come and help in the kitchen."

"I'm happy to help."

"Don't you worry! You're watching the little ones, and that's already a big help."

"It's easier when there are two. At home, Marco always wants to be near me or else he whines."

"You should have another one."

"I don't know if I can take it. It was hard at the beginning."

Bianca is always busy. She doesn't have time for sustained or precise thoughts. But now she pauses and looks at me. "You're right. No one knows how hard it is with a newborn. Not even when you've seen your mother go through it. You still can't imagine it."

If I lived here, Bianca and I would be friends.

"That's how it was for me. Already in the clinic, after he was born, I thought to myself, I'll never manage. I don't have milk, he's so small, and he depends on me completely. Then he got bigger, and the days seemed endless. I wanted to go out, go to work. I'm almost embarrassed to say it."

I stop after this outpouring of words, thoughts I had never before expressed. Now she thinks ill of me. I need to learn to be quiet.

"Please forgive me. I've never said this to anyone."

She sighs. "Now I'll tell you something I've never told anyone. If it weren't for Albert, I wouldn't have had three."

"Did he help?"

"He didn't have time to help. There's too much to do around here." Now there are red spots on her neck. "I'm embarrassed to say it."

"What better person to tell something you're ashamed of? I'm ashamed of so many things."

She takes a sip of her tisane. "One night I was in my room, breast-feeding. Albert came upstairs. The baby was pulling at the breast. My mind was elsewhere. The world could have come crashing down and I wouldn't have noticed. For days, my breasts had been sore; the baby couldn't finish all the milk. Albert stood in the doorway and watched for a while, in silence. Then he came over, picked up the baby, and put him in the crib. I looked at him without understanding what he was doing. He sat on the bed next to me. I thought, This is the boy who made me cry, who refused to talk to me. He touched my bare breast and said, 'Does it hurt?'

"'Yes, there's too much milk,' I said. 'If I can't get rid of the milk it will get infected.' He leaned over, put the nipple in his mouth, and sucked until there was no milk left. I've never felt anything like it. Even now, just remembering it, I get goose bumps; I still can't believe it happened. Christian was two months old, and that night I got pregnant with Gabriel."

LYING IN BED, I stare at the boy with the lazy eye, skiing among the flowers. Her husband sucked at her breast. I think of Manfred and the brutal way in which he tried to force me to confess. He knows the truth; he's the only one. I close my eyes. I see him in the doorway to his childhood room; he comes in, sits on the bed and undresses me, without a word. He touches my breast, puts the nipple in his mouth, and then his wet mouth penetrates mine. I remove his plaid shirt; he takes off his trousers and underwear. How often he has undressed in this room, in the cold of night or dawn.

"Time to get up, boys."

I whisper into the darkness, "Come back to bed, Manfred. It's nice and warm here next to me."

He surrenders and crawls under the covers. He's so hard, and I'm all wet; he penetrates me slowly. Then we begin to fight the same battle.

THE PIZZA WAS awful; I had to drink a lot of beer to wash it down. Stefan said the place was on the second street to the right. She's expecting me. Better, that way I don't have to talk. Her name is on the buzzer: Zara. She's Romanian. Not too young, not too old, Stefan said. A happy voice answers.

"Yes?"

"Stefan sent me."

"Third floor."

I won't be able to sleep tonight unless I have sex. She stands in the doorway, wearing a pink sweat suit. Not too skinny. Stefan knows what I like. Blond, youthful face, with a few wrinkles around the eyes.

"Come in."

Better not to look at the room, just a few details. The pillow is clean.

"Do you want a drink? No? OK."

She tries to remove my shirt, but I push her hand away. She undresses. Her underwear is pink, like her sweat suit. Not bad. I'm easily distracted. Her pubic hair is dark; she dyes her hair. She has large white breasts. She lies down on the bed, and her breasts hang on either side of her chest; she opens her legs. I focus on her belly.

After having two children, Luna's belly was no longer flat, but I still liked it. I liked to stick my tongue in her belly button, and from there I would move on to her breasts and mouth.

I undress and climb on top of her, without touching her. She wants to guide me, but I push her hand away. I put it in.

I close my eyes. Luna, come. But the dark pubis I am dreaming of is not hers. Childlike breasts, dark, frightened eyes. Thin legs wrapped around my back.

Press harder, you idiot, press harder. This is what you're good for, Marina.

12

CHILDREN'S HAIR GROWS quickly. Marco's dark hair covers the scab on his head. Today I'll wash it. It feels strange when I run my hand over the scab, like when he was small and his cranium was still soft. There's no bathroom in the room, so Bianca has offered me theirs.

Silvia lent him her bath toys; she pulls up her sleeves and rubs soap over him. I'd like to wash my hair as well. I don't have much makeup with me, just lipstick and eyeliner. No mascara, no blush. Last night I did the laundry; I washed my shirt, his T-shirt, my only pair of underwear. I left them to dry on the sink. I'm like Manfred now: one shirt, one pair of pants, always the same. He's coming up for the feast, Bianca said.

"HE'S BRINGING FOUR hikers. They'll have dinner at the lodge and then Albert will take them down in the jeep."

"Can we go down with them?"

"Wouldn't you like to stay a few more days?"

"I don't have anything with me. I left a mess down there, and I can't afford to pay for both."

She had hoped I would stay. She wants a friend, but I want to go back down to the town, even if it means I'll be alone. With Manfred downstairs. His brother has spoken with him, so I don't think he'll torment me anymore.

He saved us. What would I have done without him? His tone is harsh, but that's just how he is. I think about the power of his legs when he goes up the mountain, of his hands picking up Marco and putting him in the carrier. He knows my secret but he can't tell anyone; no one believes him. The rain is gone; today the sun is out. Marco is playing in the bath with Silvia. I'm a good mother; Bianca told me so.

"The first one is hard, but the second is easier."

"OK, LET'S GET out of the bath!"

"No."

"Won't he be cold, Silvia?"

"Yes! Come on Marco, let's go play!"

Hearing her voice, he stands up and holds out his arms so I can pull him out of the bath.

I rub him dry. He looks stronger; his face is tanned, and the shadows under his eyes are gone.

"The feast is tonight. We'll take a nap so you can eat with the grown-ups, and then we'll go into town in the jeep. It'll be fun!"

"Fun!"

Silvia and I laugh. Now that he's used to talking to the other kids, he can make himself understood.

YESTERDAY MORNING I lay on the grass, reading a book of stories about the area. I look for photos of the three boys, of their father, and suddenly I hear his voice. He speaks an entire sentence, and I can tell he's angry: "Marco ride bike alone!"

Gabriel and Christian laugh.

"You'll fall, Marco!"

"I no fall!"

His personality is changing. Mario won't recognize him. I see him as a boy, a man.

SILVIA GIVES ME Marco's T-shirt, his underwear, and asks, in a sad voice, "Are you leaving tonight?"

"Will you miss us?"

She doesn't answer.

"Maybe we'll come back once more before we leave. And soon Clara will be here."

She's lonely, like her mother. Her brothers don't want her hanging around. She liked looking after Marco.

We go downstairs. The women are preparing the tables for the evening meal. The musicians tune their instruments. Bianca comes and goes, in and out of the kitchen, greeting guests.

"I'll take the kids outside," I say.

She nods. The newly arrived guests rest in the sun on the terrace. The mountains glisten; the sun is blinding.

THE FOREST IS the point on the hike up to the lodge where everyone begins to fade. Until we reached the forest, Marina chattered and asked questions, but from there on she was short of breath and walked in silence. It's hot today, and the four hikers are sweating.

"If you like, we'll cross the stream and then we can stop to eat when we reach the moraine."

They nod. They don't even have the energy to speak. Two women and two men, around thirty-five, no children. I try to pair them off. The small woman with the tall man, two opposites; they bought their shoes in the same shop. The other two look alike. They like to cook and eat, so they're fat and they get tired. What brings people together? Chance? Or is it a certain smell, like animals? Who knows? Who destined Luna for me? No one.

I MET HER one evening when I was out with friends in the city. We were introduced: "This is Luna. She's a teacher."

She taught at the same school where we had been students. She didn't talk much. She was athletic for a teacher.

I noticed her large breasts and her muscular legs. The first impressions are the ones that stay with you.

Marina—why would anyone give their child that name?— talks a lot, wears makeup, and has thin legs. I never would have noticed her. I don't like women who wear makeup; when you touch them your fingers get dirty. Her house was filled with girls, all living with their father. At our house it was the opposite. That's why she has that ladylike air about her; she grew up with too many women. She's not used to hard work. If she were with me, I'd make her trudge up and down the mountain. Tired? Do it again. You need to be strong to raise children.

AFTER CLARA WAS born, Luna and I began to fight. Now she had a doll to play with; it wasn't the same as it had been with the boy. She chose the name. She bought clothes for her. Special treatment for the girl. I would tell her to treat Clara like her brother, but Luna couldn't help it.

"She's so little, Manfred."

It was almost as if she were talking about herself: I'm so little, Manfred, I'm a girl, I want to wear nice clothes, play house. I'm tired of this life you want me to lead.

I became impatient. After the baby was born, Luna changed, but I didn't adjust.

If you're not careful with girls, bad things happen. Just look at this one. I have the bloodstains on the tablecloth to prove it. She has to confess. Why was there blood under the table? How did the baby end up there? Marco is in danger; it might happen again. I have to tell the father, separate them.

"There is the crucifix. We can stop here and have something to eat."

They nod.

It will be hard for Marco; no matter what she does, you always want your mother. He cried when we went up the mountain without her.

"Mamma coming?"

He'll suffer, but then he'll get used to it.

THE TRAYS OF venison are in the oven, and there are sweets and crêpes on the tables. I feed Marco in a corner of the kitchen. He's tired from playing with Silvia. Gabriel pulled him around in a wheelbarrow, and he laughed until he couldn't stop.

I SEE MY sisters once a week, on Saturdays; we go to the park. We live far apart, and each of us has her activities. Sometimes I'll stay over on Sunday night with Marco. We have dinner, and I put Marco to bed with his cousins. I feel happy, as I do now. I'm overwhelmed by responsibility when I'm alone; he depends on me, and if I make a mistake it's the end. Mario doesn't understand. He's tired of the routine.

"We go every weekend!"

He thinks I act like a little girl, incapable of spending a Sunday at home, that I need to grow up. Maybe he's right. When it's just the three of us, it seems like the day lasts forever. He plays with Marco, takes him to the park while I prepare lunch, and in the afternoon we go out, or if it's raining we stay home. The baby comes between us rather than uniting us; I can feel it but I can't bring myself to explain it. Sometimes, when Mario finds me distracted and strange, he asks me, "Are you tired?"

"Exhausted."

He looks at me without knowing quite what to say.

"You wanted this baby, didn't you?"

"Yes."

"Do you love me?"

"Yes."

I have thoughts that I can't explain, all the time, with no rhyme or reason. I wanted Marco, but I didn't know. I love Mario, but I hate him because he doesn't understand.

So instead I put on music so we don't have to talk; a song from the time when we met, that way maybe everything can go back to the way it was before.

MARCO IS FALLING asleep, spoon in hand.

"Darling, you're tired, let's go to bed. You've had enough."

I pick him up and wipe his mouth. The young woman stirs the polenta and looks over.

"Are you leaving today?"

"After the party. Will there be music?"

"Of course. They eat, drink, and play. For the tourists, so they'll come up and have dinner here. Look at Marco's mountain climber cheeks."

"Yes, the mountain air has done him good."

I kiss his rough, tanned skin.

I pick up his plate and cup.

"Don't worry, I'll do it. Take him to bed; he can barely keep his eyes open."

As we go up the stairs, he puts his head on my shoulder.

When I reach the second floor I see Albert coming out of his apartment.

"Good morning, how are you?"

"Very well. He plays, sleeps, and eats."

He laughs and pinches Marco's cheek, like Manfred.

"So, the kids like it here, eh?"

"It's true."

"Tonight I'll take you down in the jeep. Bianca told me."

"Thank you."

He runs off.

Words are more important when they are few. You have to work to understand what they mean to say, really. He was referring to the first time we met, when I came into the dining room, after Manfred had left me on the mountain. I had said, "They must not have many friends to play with up here." I had almost added, "and no mother," but I didn't want them to know I had been asking about them in the town.

I wonder if Manfred still thinks about his mother; if he would like to see her, or if he hates her so much that he doesn't even think about her. I hold Marco close. How would he manage without me? If I went away, or if I died, or if they took him away from me? I wonder how they explained it to Manfred when he was little; how do you explain a mother who goes away with another man and leaves her kids?

Marco is asleep. I put him down on the bed; he never wakes up at this stage.

I have to wash my hair, and then I'll dry it with Bianca's hair dryer. My hair is long and the sink is small. When I was little, my mother used to wash my hair and dry it, and then comb it vigorously.

"You're hurting me!"

"Your hair is long, and we have to comb it, otherwise we'll have to cut it!"

I don't want to cut my hair; I like it long, and so did Marco, my first love. He was seven years old. He used to pull my hair; that was how he told me he loved me. I named my baby after him, but I didn't tell Mario. Seven is young to be in love, but I was.

I thought about him at night in bed and put my finger in the slit between my legs. My mother told me to stop.

"Your hands are dirty and it will get infected. It's delicate."

It's true, it would get all red when I rubbed it, but afterward I'd fall asleep.

The men in my life have all had names beginning with *M*. Mario, Marco. And my name, Marina.

I WRAP MY hair in a towel and put lotion on my skin. It's sunblock, the only lotion I have up here. I go over to the window. There he is, on the terrace, wearing his plaid shirt, carrying a backpack and an ice axe. He just arrived and he's looking around, speaking to a group of people, pointing to some tables and the mountain. Suddenly he looks up and sees me. I take a step back and the towel falls to the floor; I can feel the wet hair against my back.

SHE FLEES MY gaze; she's afraid. She's washing her hair, making herself beautiful. I'm hot, sweaty. The ice on the mountains is melting. I'll be more circumspect this time; I want her to fear my silence. Then I'll tell her that I was wrong about her, that she's all right. In fact, I'll act like I'm attracted to her; I'll flirt with her a little bit. That's what she wants. Then I'll wait for the right moment, when she's relaxed and vulnerable. They gave her our room, of all the rooms up at the lodge.

I go inside to talk to Albert. Bianca is at the counter, as always.

"Ciao."

"Ciao, how are you?"

"I left my clients at a table outside. Where's Albert?"

"Fixing the boiler with Christian and Gabriel. It keeps breaking down. Luckily, it's a hot day."

I walk around the house, keeping an eye on the window. But she doesn't look out; she knows I'm here.

Albert has opened up the boiler; he's struggling with the tools. Christian follows his every move. Gabriel kicks a rock.

"Ciao."

"Ciao, Uncle."

"Ciao, Manfred."

"You've got to replace that boiler."

"Maybe next year. In October I'm having the kitchen re-done. Bianca has been nagging me about it for years."

"Women are obsessed with redoing the kitchen."

Albert is a good repairman. He used to watch his father, like Christian does now. I kicked rocks, like Gabriel, and

wanted only to run off into the mountain. Maybe it was because I wore those damned glasses when I was little. My
father used to say, "With those eyes, you'll never be a mountain guide."

The more he said it the more I was determined to do it.

Albert keeps working, and then glances over. "Your friend is
happy here." He smiles mischievously.

"Who do you mean?"

"She and Bianca have become friends."

"I'm happy for her."

"Bianca likes her; she says she's straightforward, and
scared."

"I don't know her. You should ask her husband."

He laughs. "You're an odd one, brother. How is Dad?"

"He's coming up with Stefan."

"You went to visit him in town."

"Yes. He was already in his pajamas at eight."

Albert looks over at the boys. "So Stefan is wrong; he doesn't
have a girlfriend."

"Sooner or later I'll catch him."

"You're on everyone's trail, Manfred! So what if he's seeing
someone?"

"There's nothing wrong with it, but he should say so."

Albert used to be tough, but he's gone soft. Suddenly, I feel
rage rising in me. "He used to go on and on about women! He
says Stefan is right to stay unattached, and that who knows how
long Bianca will last up here!"

Christian looks at me furtively and Gabriel stops playing
with the rock. Albert stops working. He takes a dirty rag, wipes

off his hands, and says to the boys, "Go play." They run off toward the house. He speaks slowly, as he used to when something made him angry. "Manfred, how can you say that in front of the boys?"

"I wish he'd said it. At least that way we would have been prepared."

He stares at me coldly. Now I recognize my brother, the one who used to say, "Dad let someone run off with his wife."

The hardness of his eyes deflates my anger.

"Has it ever occurred to you, Manfred, that one can be more closely bound to a woman than to a brother or a father? I don't give a damn about what happened to you, to us. Don't ever bring that up again in front of my family."

His family: him, her, the three kids. The three of us, and our father—that's all over.

I WALK AWAY, but I can feel him staring after me.

I don't care about you, Albert. Or about your family, or about our father who sits around watching TV and has sex with some lady, and says about our mother: "I've talked about it with your brothers."

You can adjust however you like, but my life is fine the way it is, even without any of you.

IT'S EVENING, AND the dining room is full of voices and laughter. At a table a group of musicians eats venison ahead of the others, because soon they have to start playing. The two girls go back and forth from the kitchen. Bianca and Albert take orders, open bottles. Every so often they sit with us for a minute or two.

Bianca put us at their table. I meet Gustav, Manfred's father. His eyes are so pale that he looks almost blind. He shakes my hand and his gaze cuts right through me without seeing; he must be the same with every woman. He is seated next to me, but he has not once turned toward me. He is telling his grand-daughter Silvia about a woodchuck that used to visit him every morning when he lived here.

Stefan, the youngest, made sure to sit on my right. He tells stories about the town and pours wine.

Marco sits with the other children; Christian and Gabriel have adopted him, and he's already tired of Silvia. He wants to be with the boys.

Stefan is the most attractive of the three brothers; the woman at the pastry shop was right. He's suave; the opposite of Manfred. He talks and smiles.

"There are no new women in town; you have to travel to meet new people."

"People around here must always marry among themselves."

"Not always, but usually."

"Do you travel often?"

He has dark eyes and nice lips. He's not fair like his father and brothers. Maybe he looks like his mother; she must have been beautiful.

"I can't leave during high season because of the shop. But during the slow months, I travel."

"In Italy?"

"And other places. Last year I went to the States. Part of my family is there."

I pretend not to know. "Oh, really?"

"My mother's there, with her husband and three other kids. I rented a car and drove from the East Coast to the Pacific, and I stopped to see her."

So he went to see her.

"You have three American brothers?"

"Two brothers and a sister. All strangers, like my mother. I saw her for the first time last year."

"Amazing. How long had it been?"

"My whole life. I had no memory of her."

I turn toward his father and it occurs to me that we're talking about his ex-wife. Stefan whispers into my ear: "He doesn't hear well, don't worry."

He smiles again. He wears the mask of the ladies' man, detached and calm.

"After all, many years have passed. My mother is an old woman. She lives in a little house in the suburbs, like all the other little houses, with her famous American. Her children are grown up and live far away. Her daughter has a child. When I went to visit, they all came to meet me. In the garden behind the house, my half-sister pushed a child on the swing, and he looked just like Simon, Manfred's kid. It was quite a shock."

"Have your brothers gone to see her as well?"

"Albert and Manfred? No, Albert never goes anywhere. And Manfred is an odd duck, as I'm sure you've noticed."

I smile. "Yes, I've noticed."

"I didn't even tell him I'd gone to visit her. He wouldn't have taken it well."

I look over at Manfred, on the other side of the dining room. I've been avoiding him all evening. He is sitting with the tourists he brought up. He has his back to me, and never looks my way.

"Can I ask you something? Perhaps it's indiscreet?"

"Indiscreet? Sounds interesting."

He smiles again, and I blush.

"Did you talk, when you were there? I mean, did she explain . . ."

"How she was able to leave her three children, go away, and have three more children?"

I nod.

"She and her husband invited me over for lunch. She cooked a potato pie. Albert always asks Bianca to make it for him, and now I know why. He is the eldest, so he remembers her. To me it was just a potato pie, and not a particularly good one. The resemblance between my sister's child and Manfred's son was incredible, but so was my resemblance to my mother. A complete stranger who looks just like you. It occurred to me that it must be the same when adopted children meet their biological parents."

He takes a sip of wine. I can feel Manfred staring at me before I turn around. I turn quickly and meet his hard gaze. My heart beats fast and I lower my eyes.

Don't do that, you fool, he'll think you're afraid of him.

I look up again, but he has already turned around. Stefan is talking. I've missed the first part.

". . . they left us alone together, my mother and me, two complete strangers. She embraced me, and I pulled away. She was crying, but I wasn't very affected. I felt sorry for her because she was old. She started to say, 'I was wrong to leave you,' and other nonsense. I stopped her."

I feel uncomfortable, as if I were standing above a burning triangle. The father is staring at me; he has stopped talking to his granddaughter and listens. I'd like to make Stefan stop.

Luckily, the orchestra begins to play. The musicians have been drinking, so they play with enthusiasm. I can barely hear Stefan.

"Before I left, she said, 'Ask your father why I did it.'"

"Did you ask him?"

"Yes, not long ago. He said, 'I have no idea what she's talking about.'"

He smiles and says, almost yelling: "It's better, don't you think? Imagine if there were really a reason!"

THERE'S A NEW woman around, and Stefan is trying to impress her. Even though she's my tenant and I saved her son, and I should be the one to decide first whether I want her or not. He can't help it. It's stronger than he is. And she's willing. My brother is handsome, young, and she's ready to go. I should have sat at their table, that way I could have stopped him with a look. That's what she expected, and that's why I didn't do it.

When we crossed paths in the afternoon, I barely said hello. Marco was happy to see me.

"You want to touch the ice axe? Come here."

I barely even glanced at her. I took the tourists to the via ferrata. And now, in the dining room, I did my best not to cross her path. I didn't want to sit at the table with her and my brothers and my father. I decided that I would talk to her after dinner. I hadn't taken Stefan into account. She's sitting between him and my father. I'm not happy. She wants to become friendly with them, but tonight she's going back to town, and then we'll be alone together once again, won't we, Marina?

These four tourists only talk about food; then they eat, and talk about food some more. They exchange restaurant addresses. As soon as we're done with dinner, I'll move to the other table.

Albert and I haven't spoken, but that's OK. We've never spoken much. He thinks I see things that aren't there, that I create problems where there are none, I argue with everyone. He hasn't forgiven me for driving Luna away. When I told him she was gone, he said, "That was your only chance. You won't find another one."

It's good to have brothers.

Stefan talks and talks. What is he saying to her? The rage begins to rise again. Maybe Albert is right; I should go to the doctor and take pills. That woman irritates me; I know her like the back of my hand. Bianca doesn't get it.

"She's straightforward, and scared."

It's all a ruse. After I left her on the mountain, she came in as if nothing had happened. She's a good actress, but her act doesn't fool me. I know everything about her. She has a weak husband and she pretends to be a good mother, but she was born for something else, to make men look at her, to wear makeup and pretend to be young forever. The baby stays close to her, and she says how wonderful, his soft hands, his mouth on her neck, her breath, her shoulder. And then when you least expect it, you're dead.

STEFAN ASKS ME to dance. I've turned him down several times already. I don't want to be distracted from Marco, and I don't want Manfred to see us dancing. But he insists, and his father encourages me.

"He's a great dancer; he has even won prizes. The others are good on skis, but he's good on the dance floor."

He doesn't move his chest, his feet are light, his arms are strong, his hand on my back is delicate. He holds me close. He doesn't stop staring at me. My face is red, not because of him, but because of his brother. He has moved his chair away from the table, like the others, to watch the dancers in the middle of the room. Stefan leads me in that direction, on purpose. I don't dare look over, and in any case my head is spinning.

I can feel a torrent of hatred coming from that direction; it comes in waves every time we pass by. I know men like you, Manfred: vindictive, angry at life. You have one mission: to watch, study, know, predict.

Now I see Marco; he has climbed off his chair and is making his way through the crowd. I stop Stefan and break out of his embrace. "I'm sorry, the baby is looking for me."

I don't wait for his answer. I cross the room. Bodies twist

and turn around me and I can no longer see him. Maybe he went toward the door, maybe he went outside when no one was looking. I shouldn't have left him alone to dance around like a fool.

There he is. Manfred has stopped him and picked him up, put him on his lap and claps his hands to the music. He smiles at me as I walk over. Go ahead, take him.

Go ahead, Marina, don't be afraid. I speak loudly so he'll hear me over the music.

"Darling, are you tired? Are you tired?"

Manfred answers loudly, pretending to be jolly: "We're not tired! We're having fun watching Mamma dance, aren't we? She dances well, doesn't she, Marco? Like a young girl, and my brother knows what he's doing."

I don't look away from his pale, impertinent eyes. The baby looks at him and then at me.

"Do you dance?"

"No, unfortunately I don't know how to dance, or sing, or do lots of other nice things."

"I'm sorry to hear it! Dancing is such fun."

"Yet another thing I'll never experience in life! My mother never taught me how, did she, Marco?"

"How could she? She was gone."

I say it without thinking. It just pops out. The irony in his eyes disappears. Now he looks at me the way he did that day, when he kicked me in the kitchen.

"Who told you?"

"Your brother. She left when you were young, didn't she?" And now she lives in America.

Only you know other people's secrets, isn't that right, Manfred?

Damn that Stefan. All he does is talk, talk; he has no pride. Albert is right; he was always crying, even as a little boy.

"It must have been hard growing up here without your mother, on your own, and never seeing her again."

I reach out for Marco.

"Come on, darling, Manfred has other things to do."

He puts his arms around my neck.

"What time do you think we'll go into town?"

"I don't know," he mutters. "Ask Albert."

"It doesn't matter. If he's tired, he can sleep in the car."

I pretend to leave, and he grabs my arm tightly.

"We were just fine without her, you know."

That's your problem, you stupid little orphan. I haven't yet met the man who can trick me. I smile sweetly, gently, maternally, and pull away from his grasp.

"Especially you," I say.

"Why?"

"Stefan is not wanting for female company, as you say. He likes women, but at the same time he depends on them. And Albert, well, Bianca means a lot to him. But you are a free man. You don't need a woman, do you?"

Where are you trying to lead me? What do you want from me?

"If I need a woman, I'll find one."

"I don't doubt it. Does one of you wear glasses?"

"I do . . . I wear contact lenses. Why do you ask?"

He's the one!

"On the wall of the room where I've been sleeping there's a faded drawing of a little boy with glasses and skis. His mouth is open, and he looks sad. It touched me."

That damned drawing! I had forgotten about it.

"I never would have imagined you could be the author of that drawing."

"Why not?"

"The glasses. And the boy in the drawing is so sad, but you're strong."

"I made myself strong."

"It must have been very hard for you. I'll see you later, then."

She turns around and leaves. I don't say a word. I'd like to throttle her.

WHEN PEOPLE DANCE around you, they bump into you, and step on your toes; you don't exist for them. Stefan is talking and laughing with a woman; all he wants is company for the night. I walk up to him.

"Stefan."

He smiles. He's been drinking. "Manfred, how are you? The lady was just asking me if this is a good place for a person who doesn't know how to ski. I told her that there are great ski instructors here, don't you agree?"

The woman laughs.

"Stefan, could you come here a minute? I need to talk to you."

"Now?"

"Now."

"I'll be right back."

I lead him to the entrance, then to the veranda where we used to keep our sleds, wet shoes, and ice axes.

"Where are we going?"

I turn around to face him, filled with rage. Albert is right, everything is his fault.

"Why do you go around telling people about our lives?"

"What? What did I say?"

"You'll say anything to get a woman in bed. You'll even tell her that our mother abandoned us, just so she'll feel sorry for us!"

He laughs. "Oh, your tenant. Manfred, come on. Everybody knows!"

"Everybody! Soon they'll print it in the local guidebooks ... No one gives a damn about our story, Stefan, it's our business."

"So why are you angry?"

"I have some pride. Do you know what that is? I doubt it. Even when you were little, you were a complainer: I want Mamma, where is Mamma, when will she be back? Every day, over and over, until I threatened you, and Albert beat you up."

He stares at me without smiling. "Yes, I remember Albert's methods. And yours as well, like when you used to put my shoes outside so I had to go out in the snow in my bare feet. And then the two of you would laugh."

"I guess it didn't toughen you up much."

I've never seen Stefan like this. He never gets angry, and enjoys exasperating other people with his smile. Now he stares at me with hatred.

"You know, Manfred, I think Albert and Dad are right. I tried to defend you, but the truth is, you're sick, Manfred, and Luna was right to take the kids away. You would have made them like you."

I hit him in the face. Blood starts to pour out of his nose. He swings at me, but I dodge his fist. Now he's on top of me, and we're fighting on the ground like when we were kids, behind the house so our father couldn't see us. Now I can see his face looking out, incredulously, from the veranda, in silence. He watches us roll around.

Then Albert arrives and gets between us, separates us.

"What are you doing? There are people here! Do you want everyone to see you?"

We've regressed to twenty years ago, the fights we used to have to conceal our shame, everything hidden from the others. No one must know.

Albert opens the front door and pushes me into the night. He follows me. Behind him are Stefan and our father. They watch from the door. I'm alone outside, and the others watch from in front of the house. Albert takes three steps toward me and begins to yell, over the music from the dining room.

"You want to ruin everything, Manfred! Destroy yourself if you want, but leave us alone!"

I throw myself against him with all the force of my rage, a rage only I still feel. Albert doesn't back down; he strikes me coldly, between the cheek and eye, powerfully. When I get up, everything is a fog: his face, the house, Stefan and our father standing behind him. I've lost my contact lenses. I can hear my mother's voice: "Leave Manfred alone! You'll break his glasses!"

I used to take them off when I got into fights. But I always lost.

I can't breathe, but I can feel my heart hammering inside my chest. Albert comes close; he's not afraid, I can't hit him now.

"Get out of here, Manfred. I don't want to see you. Take your customers wherever you like, but don't bring them here. Forget this place."

Our father says nothing. Albert is in charge now.

13

IT'S DARK. THE baby is asleep in my arms and I find the keys in the umbrella stand. The house smells stuffy. The place is a mess. I empty the bathtub and put away Marco's toys, folded clothes, washed dishes, and silverware. Tomorrow the lady from the agency will come and clean.

Marco was already asleep when we climbed into the jeep. Too bad; he loves cars and motors and would have enjoyed the steep descent over the rocks.

Manfred did not return with us.

His clients were next to me in the jeep. Before we left, one of them asked Albert, "Is Manfred coming?"

Albert answered quickly. "No, he decided to walk down."

On one of the bends in the road, halfway down, the headlights illuminated his back as he walked in the dark, supporting himself with the ice axe. He didn't turn around, but I looked back at him; I wanted to see his face, but as we turned the bend he was no longer illuminated by the beam of light.

I sit at the kitchen table and reflect on the evening's events. They seem surreal, as if they had happened to someone else. The conversation with Manfred, his hostility, the idea that maybe he knows something—all of it seems to have taken place in another world. The door has been repaired, and well; there is no trace of that night.

I drink a tisane. It was easy to shame him; he was the little boy with glasses.

He hid a marker in his bed and drew the picture in the dark so his brothers couldn't see. At night he would touch the drawing with his finger before falling asleep, just as I did. The skinny little boy in short pants, with blond curls, his eyes lost behind thick lenses.

If he had been my child, I wouldn't have left him. How can you leave a little boy who doesn't speak, who never tells you what he feels, and who thinks he doesn't need anyone? You have to take him in your arms, caress him, and tell him not to be afraid, because you're there with him. Even if he doesn't speak or play; even if he's hostile and cruel, the last thing you should do is leave him. You wait for him after school, ask him a few gentle questions, kiss him even if he pulls away, make him a warm snack when he's cold, his feet are wet, and the meal at school is bad. You help him with his homework, and when he skis or plays with his brothers, you clean off his glasses. I think of what their mother said to Stefan: "Ask your father why I left." And his father's response: "I have no idea what she's talking about."

That's how it is with me and Mario. Neither of us knows what the other is thinking. We don't have the words to explain it to each other. Can I explain what happened in this kitchen? How I closed my eyes and my body, hands, and mind all went in different directions? He would be afraid of me.

Manfred saw everything. I was hiding behind the door, and he picked up Marco and took us to the hospital.

Perhaps if I'd understood him from the start, if I had seen him as I do now, a little boy with his mouth open in a scream, or walking alone on the mountain at night, leaning on his ice axe. He'll do the same when he's an old man, with less vigor. No one greets him when he comes home, neither his mother nor his wife nor his children. I could open the door for him tonight, now that the air has cleared between us and he doesn't frighten me anymore.

Take off your shoes, come in, I'll get you a beer. Did you have a nice walk? Let's sit here in the kitchen, the same kitchen from the other night. I'll tell you about my parents, my house, my sisters, the seaside, my job, and men. I'll tell you a secret I've never told anyone: I've never done anything I really wanted to, not even the baby, even though now I'm afraid they will take him away from me. I've always felt like an outsider. The thing that interests me the most is a man's love, but I've never found a man I could say it to, or even a woman. What kind of love is it if one can't tell a soul?

Manfred, I can be a good mother; even Bianca thinks so, but I want to share this terrible, crushing feeling with you, the love and hatred I feel for this child that I made.

IT'S PITCH DARK, without a sliver of a moon. I don't even have my contact lenses, but I know every stone of this road. This may be the last time I come up here; I won't return to the lodge. The moraine, the crucifix, the stream. How did the two of them come down the mountain, my mother and the man who took her away? I've asked myself many times, but I've never known.

They hold hands in the night; maybe she cries, or maybe she doesn't think at all, and he is there to support her. Can a man be everything to a woman? Can he make her forget that her children will wake up without her? It must be so, because that is what happened to us. We used to run here with my brothers, and play hide-and-seek in the trees.

"Albert, Stefan, where are you?"

This descent, and ascent, hides the secret I've been seeking for years. They've forgotten, but I can't.

I should at least have brought a flashlight. I can hear the sound of water; soon I'll be crossing the stream. There are four rocks placed close together to form a bridge. It's easy to cross there. Every spring we make sure the rocks are still there, that the current hasn't carried them away.

Everything began when that woman arrived here. The fights with my brothers, my father's silence. She wormed her way into my head, she and her child. I can't stop thinking about them; it's unfinished business.

I want to run down the mountain, go home, and smash her against a wall.

Do you think you've gotten the better of me? I have you in the palm of my hand. You know what you've done.

Now she thinks she's stronger than me. She talks to me as one does to a frightened child.

The sound of water is farther now. It happens sometimes, when it rains or after the first snowfall. I went off without thinking, my belly full of rage. I grabbed the ice axe without a word to anyone. But I should have taken a flashlight; that way, at least from close up, I could see.

I walked down too quickly, and now the stream is far away.

Once you're on the moraine, never wander from the path, and don't lose sight of the stream. If you go the wrong way, you come up to the crevasses.

All the kids in town know it. I should head back up. I can't see the mountaintops or the lights in the valley. I'll stay here till dawn, or I'll wait for the lights of the jeep on its return. I should be able to see it from here. But where am I? They passed me; maybe she was with them. Albert didn't stop.

I hear a dry sound nearby. Is it a goat, a bird, a hare? We used to be able to recognize each sound: the whistling of a woodchuck, the peep of a marten.

I've experienced this silence many times. But I was never alone; I always knew whom I would find at either end. My father or my brothers at the lodge; Luna and the kids in town. Now there's no one, neither up above where I was born nor down below where I live. I wouldn't know whom to turn to. I stand up. It's cold; I can't wait here till dawn. I walk toward the right, along the ridge, without descending, listening for the bubbling of water. I take small steps, testing the terrain. The rocks are loose; I pick one up in my hand, but it tells me nothing. I don't know where I am.

I'm not afraid of dying on the mountain. If they don't find you, even better: no coffin, no tomb. Your body breathes until the end, decomposing slowly. I speed up. I can hear the stream now; I'm going in the right direction.

A thud. What just fell? A rock moves, my foot slides, carrying the rest of my body with it. I can feel the tip of the ice axe against my side, then something pulls it away. I roll, trying to grab onto something, but nothing holds steady, everything pulls away. I can feel objects against my back, chest, shoulders, legs. Something stops me. All around me, things continue to slide. I hear soft thuds, then the patter of rocks, and then silence. Everything hurts. I close my eyes. My face is covered in dirt, but I can't clean it off. I go inside, deep down; once upon a time it was like this. A light shines, a fire.

"Warm your hands, children, but don't get too close, or you'll get burned."

IT'S ONE O'CLOCK and it's cold out. No noise on the stairs; Manfred still hasn't arrived. I can see the dark street through the window; his car is not there. Maybe he went to the city or he's drinking in town.

Why didn't he come with us? He went down alone, and he didn't turn around when we passed him. He must have left his car at the gondola station. At night it's closed. It takes a long time to go the whole way on foot. How long? Two hours from the lodge to the top of the gondola. And from there to the valley? It took us half an hour in the jeep, so it must be at least two hours on foot, or maybe one. He's fast and he knows the path by heart.

We passed him on the mountain at ten o'clock, halfway to his destination. He should be here, but the car is gone. Everything in town closes at ten, or even earlier. Where is he? It's none of my business; maybe he's with a woman. He must need to make love from time to time.

I get undressed. Marco has been sleeping well since we were up at the lodge; let's hope it lasts. I sit on the bed and put on my nightgown. On the dresser, I can see the photo with my sisters; I take it wherever I go, ever since I was a little girl. I don't know why. When I was with them, I felt less strange. I'm glad I'm not at the beach now; I needed to face the darkness inside me. It couldn't last. It would have happened again, but Manfred came in, took the child, and he doesn't believe the lies I told him. How many lies I've told. Mario would have believed me, for the sake of not knowing. It's better that it happened here.

I pick up my book and look for the bookmark, but I can't find it. I flip through the pages and turn it upside down. Where is Mario's letter? I use it to mark the page. I don't read much; I fall asleep quickly at night. I turn it over again and flip through the pages. I sit down. Who took it? Marco. It must be somewhere, under the bed or on the dresser. I move the photograph and pick up my notebook. I leaf through the pages. I see the letter tucked into the notebook before the last page. Who put it there? He did. He came in when the carpenter came to fix the door, dug around, and read it. My eyes scan the letter.

I look at the clock, get up, return to the kitchen, peer out of the window. The car is still not there. He came into my apartment, went through my things. Strangely it does not make me upset, only sorry that the place was such a mess. What he already thought, he is now sure of. That I'm worthless as a woman and as a mother.

Why hasn't he come back?

Once again, I go over the path he must have taken. After walking for three hours at night, you don't go out on the town in your car. I've always seen the car parked in front of the house, since my arrival. It seems strange that on this particular night, after walking down the mountain, he should decide to go out. I sit at the table. Maybe I should call the police, tell someone. They'll take me for a fool for thinking that a mountain guide could get lost on the mountain in his own backyard.

Why didn't he accompany the tourists he had led up the mountain? When the headlights illuminated his neck, he didn't turn around. If I call the police, they'll think something strange is afoot. They won't believe me; they'll think I'm crazy. If Manfred told them what he saw that night, they'll think he was telling the truth. I won't call.

He was here, in every room, searching, looking, digging. I wish at least I had emptied the tub and washed the breakfast dishes. No one has ever hounded me as he has; he's on my trail and he won't let go. Neither will I. I'm calling the police; I don't care if they think I'm crazy.

THE SNOW QUEEN. The chapel, and its altar with empty vases, the benches, the heater that no one ever turns on. Everything is out of focus. I've carried the injured and the dead here, in summer and in winter. Now it's my turn. We keep dead bodies here while we wait for them to be identified. I'm alone. No one has come yet to claim me.

I remember lights, torches, searchlights, hands pulling me upward, the rods of the stretcher digging into my flesh. Then the air, and the sky coming closer; the feeling of being lifted onto something, rising in the air, screaming with each lurching movement. Nothing comes out of my mouth. I don't hear words, just screams, dogs panting, and the vortex of the helicopter blades above everything. Then the pain stops—perhaps I'm dead—and they carry me to the chapel.

I try to move my head, but I can't. Something is holding my neck in place. Blurry faces. I don't recognize them. They speak quietly. How gentle they all are. I'd like to tell them: I'm short-sighted, come closer.

But the faces disappear, and then I'm moving again. I close my eyes; better to look inside of myself, and focus on the fire. Where am I?

A bonfire at night. My mother holds me and says, "Warm yourselves! But don't go too close, or you'll get burned."

We warm our hands at the fire, and I put my hands in hers; she squeezes them. I'm warm, inside and out.

SITTING ON A bench in the park, I watch them play. Marco and Bianca's children. All the adults are in the hospital, where he is being operated on. His wife and children are on their way.

I called the police. I stammered, not knowing quite what to say.

"I'm not sure, and I'm probably mistaken. We passed him on the way down, but he hasn't arrived yet. I don't have the number of the lodge, but it might be a good idea to call his brother."

I leave my number, hang up, and wonder whether I've made a fool of myself. I think of how he'll laugh when he finds out. I climb into bed but I can't sleep. The phone doesn't ring. I turn off the light. I make fun of myself, as I always do when I feel that I've done something dumb, to comfort myself.

You're an idiot, you're crazy. You just told the police to call his brother. They'll call Manfred, and he's probably in bed with a woman or somewhere else. When he returns tomorrow, I won't be able to look him in the face. He'll think I missed him, that I was worried about him. As soon as he sees me he'll start laughing. The whole town will laugh: Bianca, his brothers, his father.

I toss and turn in bed as I talk to myself. Then, in the middle of the night, I hear an ambulance siren. I get up, go to the kitchen, and open the window. The siren wails in the distance; I can hear the hum of a helicopter in the mountains. It barely occurs to me that it might be for him. In the dark sky the helicopter circles above the gondola station. The town begins to awaken and lights come on in the windows. The telephone rings.

"They found him at the bottom of a crevasse. They're taking him to the hospital."

I tell myself: you saved him. But I don't believe it.

This morning, Bianca left the kids with me and went to the hospital with Albert. She says they will have to put a metal plate on his spine, at chest height.

How will he work with a metal plate on his spine? Better not to think about it. Maybe his wife will come and take care of him.

I feel a strange calm. Marco runs in the park, followed by Gabriel. He looks bigger; soon he'll be a boy like those two. Mario will find him changed; will he see something new in me as well?

In a week I'll be at the beach, and I'll forget Manfred. I could have invited him into my bed, just once, before Mario and Manfred's wife arrived. Who would have known? What would it have changed? For the others, nothing. For us it would have been something different, something crazy. We're already crazy. Why am I thinking about this while he's in the operating room and they're putting a metal plate on his spine? I should be hoping that the operation goes well and that his wife will take him back.

THIS IS ALL I want: to spend a single night with him. Even if he's brutal, rushed, or who knows what else, I want to try. Then everything can begin again: Mario, Marco, my sisters, the sea. He can go back to his wife, and everybody will be happy. Once, just once, I want to feel those hands—the hands that picked up Marco, put him in the backpack—pulling down my trousers, undoing my bra. I want to feel goose bumps where he touches me, and to kiss him.

Afterward I'll dance slowly in front of you, naked, in silence. You can whisper in my ear, even terrible things, tell me what you think, everything. And I won't be tender. We'll tell each other the truth. Finally, someone to whom we can tell the truth.

I want to hear about your mother, Manfred, or if you prefer, I can tell you a story. The American arrives one day; he's handsome, different, and talks more than your father does. Before his arrival, she didn't know how much she hated you. Don't get angry, wait, be calm. She loved you, but at the end of the day, when she put you to bed and the sun set, and she had finished everything, she would undress, and your father would look at her. "Are you happy?"

And then she would hate you. Happiness, despair, it means nothing, Manfred. You kicked me when I was sitting behind the door, to make me get up. That's how it is when you have a child; life kicks you in the gut. You try to shield yourself, you think you can avoid it. But if you know that's how it is, you just take it, you put on a brave face, you love and you hate, because that's what you have to do. You just have to know. Now I know, because I met you.

We make love again. We call it that, but between us, it's not love, it's something else.

MY EYELIDS ARE heavy. I open my eyes, then close them again. There is a tube in my mouth. I can't move my head, so I move my eyes instead. There is a blurry face nearby, something near my ear. A metallic voice speaks slowly, clearly pronouncing each syllable.

"How do you feel? It's me, Luna. Your father is here, and your brothers, and the kids. Soon you'll be back home. Stay calm. You fell, and the woman living in the apartment upstairs called the police. They found you and operated on you. Everything will be all right. We're here."

The blurry face moves away.

I think about the words she said, one by one.

Luna, the kids; I've fallen; I've been operated on. The woman upstairs called the police.

Marina. Of course. Falling, rocks, pain. I feel nothing. My thoughts begin to come back to me. The distant rage, like the thunder after an avalanche.

Marina called the police. Where is she? No, she's not here. She's at home with the baby. Her husband is coming to get her. She saved herself from me, she raised the alarm, she saved me.

Marina.

I articulate her name. She's clever; now she'll take advantage of what's happened and leave all this behind. I have to be thankful. Just wait till I'm better, I won't give up; she'll tell the truth. I have the proof on the tablecloth. Where did I put it? In my trouser pocket. It won't end here. She's much cleverer than Luna; she shoved the story of my mother in my face.

Luna never mentioned her; she was too afraid of my reaction. She would tell the kids that Grandma lived far away and that one day they would go see her. Clara told me.

Simon and Clara are here; it must be serious.

"Everything will be all right."

That's what they always say. I should consider this: I was operated on, maybe I'll die, or I won't be able to move, or I'll be a vegetable. And her? She'll get away with it and go off with her husband. Maybe I'm already a vegetable and I don't even know it. Someone who is about to die and can only think about how to make trouble for that woman has a few screws loose.

I think about her husband loading up the car, kissing her. "How have you been? And the baby?"

She pretends to be an angel, a sweet little mamma. I can't stand the idea, even if I'm half dead. Manfred, you're cooked, full of pills, and not making any sense. Once you're dead, what do you care? No, I want to see her cry, plead, apologize, throw herself on the floor, kiss my hands, beg me. Maybe I'm already dead, these are the thoughts of a dead man. Who says dead men are at peace?

On the contrary, they can finally give free rein to their rage, say everything, curse whomever they please.

I'll make you come here, Marina.

Climb up on the bed, come closer or I can't see you. I'm shortsighted, as you know. Look at me now. You feel sorry for me, don't you? You can remove the tube from my mouth. Do I disgust you? That way I can tell you what you are. Come close, and I'll run my fingers through your hair. You washed it, you put on makeup; whom were you trying to seduce? Everyone; the first man who comes along can take you. I don't want you. I don't care if you dance and try to impress me. I saw you on your knees behind the door; I kicked you because you wouldn't get up and go to him. You want to leave but you can't; stay here until I wake up, while I still want you, until you've done your time. Stay here, I'll fuck you and you'll see, I won't die.

14

M AY I COME in?"
          "Yes, of course."
She holds out her hand.
"I'm Luna, Manfred's wife."
"Marina."
"The kids are sleeping. Yours too?"
I nod. She looks around at the apartment. She's a beautiful woman, large, tall, with broad shoulders, large breasts, a wide face, and light almond-shaped eyes. She doesn't look terribly young, around forty I would say, like Manfred.

"I haven't been in here for years. I decorated this apartment. A carpenter used to live here, and it looked like a toolshed. Everything was old, and it was full of stuff; he never got rid of anything. My father-in-law bought the house, both apartments, and when we got married he gave them to us."

"It's comfortable, we've been happy here. Would you like to sit in the kitchen? I was having a tisane; would you like one? Or would you prefer a glass of wine?"

"A tisane would be lovely, thank you."

She sits down at the table and looks around with a proprietary air, as if checking to see whether everything is as she left it. Luckily I've done the dishes. I take a cup and pour the tea. It's strange, serving this woman in her own house.

"I wanted to thank you for making the call."

I sit across from her. She has strong, rough hands. Her face looks tired, like Bianca's. Heavy work and cold air, and they don't do much to protect their skin.

"I don't know how I got up the nerve to call. He could have been out somewhere."

She smiles stiffly. "Manfred hardly ever goes out. At least that's how it was when we were together. He goes to bed early."

"At one in the morning I looked out and the car still wasn't there."

She stares at me. There is something she wants to know. I blush and look down, like an idiot.

"Do you usually go to bed late?"

"No, not usually." Marina, be careful, don't say anything stupid. "But ever since the accident, and our time up at the lodge, the baby has been sleeping more soundly and I've been going to bed later."

"The accident?"

What does that have to do with anything? Why did I bring it up?

"He fell off the table."

She listens, staring at me all the while.

"Your husband . . . Manfred . . . drove us to the hospital."

There you go, you've told her everything, as if you needed to justify yourself.

She smiles, but there is still something hard about her. I smile too, as I used to do in school, hoping she'll like me. After all, she's a teacher.

"Are you from around here? A teacher?"

"Yes, I teach in the city. Did Manfred tell you?"

She's diffident.

"No, Bianca told me."

That's better: short answers. Don't embellish. Do as she does. She drinks her tea. Now she has a vague look on her face. I don't want to ask her how he is; Bianca already told me.

"The rehabilitation will take a long time, but he'll be all right, though not like before. He'll need help; he'll have to live with someone."

Silence. Tears stream down his wife's face. She cries openly, without moving. Maybe he is in trouble.

My voice trembles. "Please don't cry . . . Bianca told me that he'll be able to walk, and do almost everything he does now."

She wipes her tears away with her hand. What drama this kitchen has seen!

Dishes decorated with little trees; cups decorated with squirrels, all chosen by her; edelweiss on the potholders, embroidered place mats, doilies, curtains, a perfect setting for a tragedy. I'd like to tell her that we should destroy everything and begin again.

She speaks slowly. Her strength, the accumulated effort, everything disappears. "I don't know if I'll be able to manage."

I think she means the effort of coming back, taking care of him.

"He could go live with one of his brothers. You have your life, and the accident is a separate matter, isn't it?"

Perhaps it's better if they don't get back together. I prefer to think of him alone than with her.

"No other man moves me the way he does."

I'd like to go back to the way we were before the tears. She is a strong woman; why has she decided to confide in me? I don't want to hear about the two of them.

"I would have stayed with him. He's a difficult man; when he is convinced of something there is no way to make him change his mind."

"I've noticed."

She looks up at me, but it's not me she's interested in; she wants to empty herself in front of this woman she doesn't know, who saved her ex-husband's life.

"I don't care about that, about his difficult personality, or the kids who don't want to be with him. He is their father, and they must come to terms with him. In our house, they have a picture of him in their room. The boy, the one who didn't get along with him, put it there. Clara talks about him less. But Simon is obsessed with his father."

She shakes her head and looks at me. "I didn't leave because of them, because of the violent scenes, and I wouldn't go back to him just because of the children."

I interrupt her; I don't want to create an intimacy with this woman. "I barely know Manfred . . . he seems like a difficult man. I understand that he must be hard to live with."

"Is there a man who is not difficult to live with?"

I don't know what to say, or where this conversation is heading. "It all depends. Everything was easy with my husband until the baby was born; then things became more complicated. Maybe it was my fault, who knows."

She sighs. "The first few years, we were happy, even after Simon was born. But after Clara was born, he became touchy and impatient. Clara's birth changed everything."

"In what way?"

"Clara reminded me of my mother, even as a little girl. I spent days with her in my arms, and I felt more vulnerable."

She plays with the spoon in the empty cup. "I wanted to be with him, but I couldn't be as I had been before."

She stops speaking and looks at me. "I don't want to bore you."

"Don't worry, I like listening to you talk."

I don't know if this is really true, but I do feel sorry for her.

"I felt so alone downstairs just now, with the children asleep. I started to think about so many things. Everything looks so neglected, uncared for. He threw away every single object I had bought; every single one. It's almost as if a woman had never lived there. I've been erased."

"How is that possible? You lived together for many years."

She answers me with an exalted expression. "Bianca thinks I left because of that time he hit me."

"He hit you?"

So you too have things to hide, Manfred.

"After one of our arguments. But that's not the only reason. I left because of the way he looked at me when I was holding the baby, when I was with her. It scared me. That look on his face . . . I couldn't stand it. I would provoke him, so the ugliness would come out; I already knew what he thought of her, and of me."

"Of the child?"

"Yes, her too. He thought we had betrayed him."

I saw her sitting there, in this new house, reflecting on the past: the arguments, the misunderstandings. The children are sleeping, some nights she longs for her husband, but the vessel is broken. She runs a finger under her moist eye.

"Manfred is not completely wrong—after all, in a way I did take him for a ride."

"Why do you say that? We all change."

She gets up, takes the cup to the sink. Now she is at home, and I am the guest.

"The first few years I really believed in all of it, and I wanted him so much I would have done anything to have him. I went hiking up in the mountain, and he taught me many things. I wanted him; the rest didn't matter. I still want him, but I don't think I'm up to . . ." she pauses, ". . . to being carved out of wood."

I peer at her without understanding.

"Have you ever been downstairs? The only thing he has kept is a sculpture he had made when we were engaged, of our faces carved out of the same piece of wood. He keeps it by the fireplace."

"He's crazy!"

She smiles. This time she is really amused. "A little, yes. I should go."

I get up, follow her. She stops at the door and says, "Who knows what will happen now, after the accident. Maybe he'll need me."

The idea that they might get together because of his infirmity irritates me. "Do you really think people can change?" I ask.

"You said it yourself."

I'm mumbling. "Yes, but Manfred is very rigid."

She is wearing the same inquisitive look as when she arrived. "When are you leaving us?"

"Me? At the end of the week. My husband is coming for me. Why?"

"Manfred asked if you could come and visit him before leaving." As she says this, she looks me squarely in the eye. I blush. Luckily the entryway is dark. "You can leave the child with me; there's a garden at the hospital."

"Yes, I know, I was there."

I CAN'T STAND it. All of them standing around me, smiling sweetly.

"Do you want a glass of water? Does the wound hurt? Is the catheter all right?"

I wish they would get out of here and leave me alone. They make small talk. Luna talks about the kids.

"They want to know how you are."

Bullshit. Children don't want to hear about sick parents, or absent ones for that matter.

Albert and Stefan try to tell me where to live. They want to hire a male nurse to take care of me.

"Why don't you go and stay with Dad? He'll be happy, and it will be easier to find a nurse in the city."

I wave my hands, making clear signs that everyone can understand.

Quiet! I don't want to hear it!

As soon as they forget about me I'll go home and find a woman to come help. Maybe she'll be young and willing, that way I can solve two problems at once. I'll need someone.

After the operation, the doctor came into the room. He asked everyone to leave, and explained the situation. It was the same doctor from when Clara broke her arm. A straight shooter.

"Manfred, you have a fracture between your thoracic spine and your lumbar spine, but luckily the spinal medulla is intact. We've done what we can, and we'll see how bad the damage is over time."

My brothers don't come anymore, nor does my father. As soon as I could talk, I told them I didn't want visits. My throat hurt, it was hard to speak, but I wanted to make certain things clear.

"I won't come up to the lodge, but I don't want to see you here either. I don't need anyone."

They come to the hospital anyway, but they stay downstairs and talk among themselves, and then ask Luna how I'm doing. It's harder to send her away, though I've tried.

"Go on vacation with the kids. I don't need you."

As soon as I said it, she started to cry. It's tiring to lie still on the bed and watch her cry. She never used to cry, and she would swallow her tears whenever we had a fight.

"I don't want to lose you, Manfred. I realize it now, after being apart."

I try to convince her, but it's hard to argue when you're lying down.

"You didn't even want to come here with the kids."

"I was afraid to see you. These nights since I've been home with the kids, I've realized how much I missed you, and how much you've missed me as well."

She's wrong. All I wanted was her body. I don't tell her, or she'll start to cry again.

"Stop that. Help me change."

I take off my glasses, that way I can't see her. She brought them to the hospital, as well as clean underwear every day, and sweets I don't eat. She changes me and combs my hair, like a child. She dominates me. Her hands rub soap on my skin, and I enjoy it, it's pleasant, but I don't want her. Better than a stranger, of course, and maybe with time the desire might come back. And that way I would have the kids near me.

They came to see me the other day. Clara gave me a kiss, but not Simon. Luna encouraged him, but he just stared at me. I told her to stop.

"Leave him alone."

I could have Simon and Clara back, bug them, watch them grow, take them up the mountain. But there would be fights, and rage, like before. I don't know if I could handle it. She rolls me over and whispers to me.

"If it's true that you don't miss me, then why did you keep the sculpture?"

I was waiting for winter to burn it in the fireplace.

If I weren't injured and she didn't cry at the slightest excuse, that would have been my answer.

But instead I say nothing; it's not worth it. I want to feel better. The pain medication helps until lunchtime, but then the pain returns, and they can't give me too much.

"When is she coming?"

"She's here. Wait, I'll go down."

That's right, I need to see her alone. But how does Luna know?

She puts me in a reclining position and whispers, "She's leaving the boy with me, that way she can come up by herself."

Our thoughts still hear each other; when you've been married for a long time, it happens.

She's here. She'll see what I've prepared for her. She thinks I'm out of the way, that she's free now. No one can put one over on Manfred.

Luna finishes cleaning me and makes the bed. She's good at putting things in order. She puts my hands on the sheet, but I stop her.

"I'm not dead yet."

"Manfred!"

I've always enjoyed frightening her. I put on my glasses. She picks up the dirty laundry. In the doorway she turns around.

"Do you need anything?"

"No, ask her to come up."

She stares at me. "Are you attracted to her, Manfred?"

I pretend not to react. Before she left, when we no longer had sex and I wandered off to get laid wherever I could, she always knew, as soon as I came in the door.

"She saved my life. Don't you think I need to thank her?"

"Don't get upset, it's not good for you."

It didn't take much to convince her, even before. Typical Luna. She never really wanted to get to the bottom of things.

The white door is closed. She sees me in my glasses, and thinks of the drawing on the wall. Who cares; I know how to intimidate her. I'm thinking of Marco, after all. But no, I shouldn't pretend, it's her. What a show she put on at the lodge; she washed her hair and danced with Stefan while the boy looked for her, and then she tossed out, "Didn't your mother leave you?"

I'm filled with rage, I'd like to strangle her, but I don't have the strength. I have to calibrate carefully what I can do and say, so she'll be scared. She'll try to light a fire and then change the subject, talk about the drawing on the wall or my current state. That's when I want to kill her. I mustn't let her lead me by the nose. I have a different game to play. Silence, a few words, a look; I'll wait in silence, and she will be devoured by curiosity and fear. She wants to know who you are, but you never tell her the whole truth, you don't put yourself in her hands, you're always one step ahead, like that day on the mountain. You carried off her boy and made her sweat. You may not have the strength in your body, but in your mind, yes. Come, Marina, I'm waiting for you.

I KNOW THESE benches; I recognize them from the other time we came. They were empty then, it was nighttime, and I was carrying my baby in my arms. Now there are patients in hospital gowns, sitting or walking in the park. Everything seems to end up here, at this hospital.

Luna tries to keep Marco with her, but he fusses. He starts to cry.

"I want my mamma."

"I'm going to see Manfred, darling. I'll be back in a minute. I told you, he fell."

Luna pulls out a bag of candy and whispers, "I'll give you all the candies you want; we won't tell Mamma."

He looks at me, smiles slyly, and accepts the deal. They walk away together. Children are terribly malleable; they believe anything we tell them.

I push open the glass doors.

THE MORNING AFTER giving birth, they brought the baby to me so I could breast-feed him. I didn't know yet that I didn't have milk. My mother, Mario, and his relatives hadn't arrived yet. It was just the two of us.

I looked at him and felt an immense strength. I made him; one day, he will become a man. When I'm dead, this tiny thing will be a giant. I will help him grow. Then, for days, months, years, I forgot about that moment.

I GO UP the stairs to the second floor, Room 20. I'm afraid that I will be shocked by what I see. Luna says it's not so bad.

"He's all right; he doesn't feel much pain. He can't move, but he can speak. He's not giving up, you know how he is."

"How do you mean?"

"You'll see."

The hallway is empty and the door to his room is closed. My heart is pounding. Why? Marina, this man has been battling against you since the very first day, but no one, not a soul, knows you the way he does, or ever has. Be on your guard. If he wants to thank you, just say, "It was the least I could do."

That's it. Tomorrow Mario comes for you, and all this will be over. The fear, the desire, the beating of your heart. You mustn't tell a soul, Marina, or even think it, because he'll see it in your eyes; if he understands how much you desire him he'll have you in the palm of his hand. Close your heart; be distant, strong, and cold.

THE WHITE DOOR opens. The same ice, on either side.

There she is. A beautiful woman, but not your type.

THAT'S HOW I like him: lying down, clean, wearing his glasses. Now what do I say?

"How are you?"

She uses the familiar *tu*, as I did that night, when I broke down the door.

"I could have died, but I'm still here."

"Should I sit down?"

I nod. From the bed, she looks small and thin. I wonder how she sees me?

He looks like the boy in the drawing. Don't feel sorry for him, Marina.

Don't feel sorry for her, Manfred.

"I want to thank you for calling the police."

"It was the least I could do."

"Why?"

What should I say? "You know why."

He smiles; I'm afraid of what he will say. I want to climb into the bed with you, Manfred. There's no one around. We can hold each other close; we don't need to talk.

"You mean because I brought Marco here that night?"

She nods. Now I'll wait a moment, so she thinks she's off the hook.

His rough hand lies forgotten on the sheet. Will it be strong again, as it was before? Otherwise, what was the use of calling the police? He stares at me with a serious air.

"From you."

"From me what?"

"I saved him from you."

If I run out of this room, who will stop me? Not he; he can't move.

"I know that's what you think. But it's not true."

"No?"

I feel tired, like when I was a little girl, when I got into trouble. You're not free; the baby cries, you can't take it. It's hard for you; no one knows but him. And then one day the darkness returns, the silence, the icy cold.

Don't say a word. She's beginning to crack, just wait.

"What do you want from me, Manfred?"

"I don't know. You tell me."

I feel I'm about to cry. I can't let him see me weaken.

"Do you want to take him away from me?"

"Should I?"

You've always known that you are different from other women, Marina. You don't know how to be a mother. Just say it.

"Yes, I've known it ever since he was born. I love him, but it means nothing because at times I feel that I hate him. Sometimes I'd like to go away, give him away to the first person I see, but he only wants me, he waits for me and cries if he doesn't see me."

"All babies are like that."

"Yes, but I can't handle it. I try with all my might but I can't do it. Suddenly I feel overwhelmed, but there's no way out. When you have a child, it's like that all the time. But I can forget about him at times, think of other things."

"Like dancing."

He's crazy. What is he talking about? Oh God, what have I said? I've let myself fall into his trap; what have I done?

I get up and walk to the door.

"Wait."

I turn around. He smiles. He's a monster.

"You want to get rid of him, don't you?"

I walk toward the bed, my hand raised in a fist.

"You're crazy! Luna said you were."

He stops my hand with his.

"Hit me if you like, but don't yell. The nurses will hear you."

I lower my hand, but he doesn't let go. I let my hand slide down into his; he holds it tight, as he did at the stream. We stare at each other, both thinking the same thing: an emptiness in our bellies, a feeling of weakness. We're both overwhelmed.

"Your husband is coming for you."

"Tomorrow."

He has me in the palm of his hand, just as he always has. He's the only one who ever has.

I lean over him without realizing what I'm doing. I part his lips with mine, and he lets me. I feel his tongue, the saliva, the inside of his mouth.

I want this woman; she's the only one I want. I need to find the strength to tell her.

"Don't leave me."

I pull away and kiss him lightly once more. A tender kiss, like the kisses I give Marco. My cheek touches his. He whispers into my ear, "Don't leave the boy."

The Return

1

I THINK BACK TO who I was fifteen years ago, when I came here for the first time, and I can barely recognize myself. It's almost as if that woman—alone, on vacation with her first child—were not me at all. Peering out of the train, I sow my thoughts across the expanse of snow.

MARCO IN HIS stroller. I push him around, under the mountains, at dawn. I'm cold; always, cold and tired. The cows in the field, his ice axe in the entryway, mud from his boots on the floor. Everything is jumbled together: feelings, fears, desire. I trudged up the mountain, and inside of myself.

Many times I've thought of giving you the gift of these years, Manfred. Look at me now. And Marco; I think you'd like to see what he's become. Always angry, with me, with his father;

when he goes out you never know when he'll be back. On the weekends, he sleeps like the dead. At one in the afternoon, I peer into his room to see if he's breathing; when he was a baby, he never slept. He doesn't talk much, and doesn't appreciate a lot of talk. He studies hard, and he's never happy.

I have a daughter, Manfred, three years younger than Marco. When she was born, I didn't want to listen to anyone. No advice, thank you very much. I breast-fed her for four months. Her name is Silvia, like Bianca's daughter. I tried to give her the strength I didn't have. She holds her own against her brother, and argues with me, but she's more accommodating with her father. And she loves to dance.

Many times, I've wondered what your daughter is like now. And the little ones? They must be more than twenty years old.

I haven't tried to keep in touch these fifteen years. I wrote you a letter, a week after I left. It came back to me. You mailed it back to me in another envelope with my address on it, so I would know you had read it. No comment, just like Marco. I don't know anything about your life, but I've thought about you, dreamed about you, spoken to you.

More than anything: desire. The first few years, it made me cry in bed. I felt a pain in my stomach, even on the morning Silvia was born, at the hospital. Come now, I thought, come through that door, I want you to see her. Once again I've become a mother.

You didn't come, you never did, but you were always there. The emptiness in my belly became a memory. No more pain; it kept me company.

⌒

"A LONG TIME ago, almost fifteen years ago, I met a man. I feel like I knew him more than any other man in my life." I told one of my sisters, the youngest. She had lost her husband in an accident, and was raising her children alone. She was inconsolable.

"You had a lover?"

"I wanted to make love to him, I won't lie, but it never happened. He knows something about me that no one else knows. I never saw him again, but he never left me. He kicked me, picked me up, and returned Marco to me forever. I know what you'll say; that's why I've never told anyone. You'll say: you never lived with him, shared a life, children. What do you know about him? Nothing; I don't even know whether he can walk, or whether he's with his wife or with another woman. But I know he's alive."

She smiled sadly.

"My husband is alive every morning when I wake up, and then he dies again a second later."

"That's why I'm telling you. Presence and absence: sometimes it's difficult to distinguish between the two."

She hugged me and then ran off to take the children to school. Maybe it helped her, who knows.

I SEE THE mountains. I'm afraid. Three more hours and I'll be there. Maybe you've left, gone to Alaska. I've considered that possibility. But it's enough to see the house and go up to the lodge. Do Bianca's children run it now? Maybe they're all gone, but I don't think so. Hard to imagine that the Sanes could leave these rocks, the stream, the woods.

THEY PARK THEIR cars every which way. It snows, and they don't move them. You dig out the tires, spread gravel, but it's pointless: they just don't know how to maneuver in the snow.

"Don't rev the engine, softly now, don't turn the wheel too sharply."

But they can't do it. They come from the city, and they don't know how to drive. They say, "Could you do it, please?"

Can't they see my leg? Don't they know I can't drive? They apologize.

"It's all right. Try again. Not too much gas, easy now."

They can't do it, and I have to call Simon and the cook and ask them to push.

I'd like to hurl insults at them, but I can't. They are our customers. Luna has taught me to be nice.

"We have to pay the mortgage."

The mortgage has changed my life. She agrees: "You've improved, Manfred, you're almost normal now."

What choice do I have?

"The hotel is doing better than your brother's lodge, or than Stefan's business. You should be happy!"

We do it for Clara, who is studying in the city, and for Simon, who will take over the business when we're old. Or tired. I'm already tired. I try to get out as often as possible, to do repairs, shovel snow, discuss plans and bills. I look up at the three-story hotel which was once my house.

Once a week I hike up the mountain on my own. I walk slowly, with a cane, without being seen. I keep the good leg fit. It's even stronger now, the muscles are hardened and it works for two; my customers don't even notice my bad leg.

I leave the shovel next to the garage; I'll do the rest later, when everyone is on the ski slopes.

I brush off the shoes by the door. When my father died, we took back the rug. Luna put it here in the entryway, next to the bench. Every time I come in, I think of him. Simon is on the phone with his girlfriend, who lives in the city. I torment him a bit about her; I don't want them to get married too soon.

"Where is your mother?"

He points toward the kitchen and says into the phone, "Hold on a minute."

"Room 10 called. The shower is acting up."

"I'll go look. Get off the phone."

"OK, Pop."

He swallows his words; he must be imitating something from TV. It doesn't bother me.

"Manfred, do you realize you've only said three words all day? I'm not exaggerating; exactly three."

I talk less and less; maybe it's some sort of disease. Or maybe I have nothing to say. I wonder if there is anything left to add, but I can't think of anything.

Up on the mountain, when I sit down to eat a sandwich and have a beer, in silence, I would like to have someone to talk to.

Once I screamed, just to hear my own voice, and then I started to laugh. I felt like I was trying to call someone.

I don't feel like talking. Luna has too much work to do to complain or feel lonely. The kids know what I'm like, but I make an effort, especially with Clara, when she comes home for the holidays.

"Do you enjoy school?"

"Of course." Clara is brusque, not like when she was a kid and she tried to keep me happy so I wouldn't get mad. "I don't want to live here, and I don't want to look after the hotel."

"You're right. You should do what you want to do."

My acquiescence irritates her; she likes to do battle, like me. She looks like me too. But I don't want to fight. Maybe all that rage died, along with this leg that I drag behind me. Luna is right: since the accident, I've changed.

I go up the stairs to Room 10, on the third floor, and knock on the door. They've gone out. The bed is unmade, clothes on the chairs. I go into the bathroom to fix the shower. I need to change the washer, so I take the shower apart and leave it on the basin; as I turn, I catch my reflection in the mirror. You've aged, Manfred. The news of the day is: the shower in Room 10 is leaking. The rooms are completely different now; the architect has created showers, bedrooms, hallways, added doors, knocked down walls, built partitions. The house is unrecognizable.

"HAVE YOU BEEN here before?"

"Once, a long time ago."

The young woman leads the way. "The town hasn't changed much."

"I noticed. The pastry shop is still in the same spot, and so is the bakery and the butcher's. Fifteen years ago I rented an apartment on the road that leads up to the large meadow."

She opens the door. The room is small, and the windows look down on the piazza. I put down my suitcase, open the curtain, and see the tables and the band. It's the day of the town fair.

"Is the room all right?"

I turn around. "Yes, it's lovely. The place I rented back then belonged to Manfred Sane."

"He runs a hotel now."

Maybe she means someone else. In small towns, sometimes several people have the same name.

"His brother used to run the lodge up at the pass."

"Albert. He still does."

Over the years I've imagined him here, or on the mountain, or traveling, alone, with his wife, or with someone else, but I never imagined him running a hotel.

"Does he actually run the hotel?"

"Yes, with his wife and son."

With his wife; I should have guessed. Marina, that's not what you wanted. You just wanted to see him again, that's all.

In the doorway the girl asks, "Are you staying one night?"

"Yes, I'd like to go up to the lodge tomorrow. Is it open? Can I stay there?"

"Yes, of course. If you'd like, I can call. They'll come pick you up with the snowcat at the gondola station."

I sit down on the bed. "I'll think about it and let you know at dinnertime."

I'm alone now. The house has become a hotel, and he runs it, like his brother, with his wife. You've lived with your husband for fifteen years; you have a daughter, a new house, you've traveled a bit.

I lie down on the bed. I should unpack; dinner is early up here. I close my eyes. There was a reason why I returned, a fantasy I had entertained all these years.

IN BED AT night, the light on my side is off. Mario reads.

Nighttime, darkness, cold. I hurt my baby boy when he was very little. He doesn't remember, or maybe some part of him, deep inside, still does. Manfred is the only one who knows, and yet he is the one who entrusted me with the boy. That is why I was able to raise him, and why Mario is still with me.

In my fantasy, I go back, to see how he's doing and whether he is able to walk. I bring him a photo of the kids, we talk. After all, we spoke so little back then. I take a train by myself, without telling him I'm coming. I book a hotel and call him from there. We see each other. I'm older, and so is he, and so we are finally able to transform our desire into words.

I SIT UP, open the suitcase, and pull out a few things. Tomorrow I'll go up to the lodge and see Bianca and Albert. Then, when I'm ready, I'll see him as well.

I WALK BETWEEN the tables, looking for Luna. A few of the newer guests notice my limp; the others know already.

"Good evening, Manfred. The snow was stupendous today."

"I'm so glad."

"What will the weather be like tomorrow?"

They ask me every night.

"Cloudy, but it won't snow."

I'm guessing, but I'm usually right.

Luna stands at a table, talking to a group of guests. She's good at talking to people; they are drawn to her, and they come back. I wouldn't get far with the hotel on my own, but after all she was the one who wanted the place. I wait for her to finish. She describes the ski runs, where to go for the ski pass, how to rent skis. How can she stand to say the same things over and over, and always with a smile? She was a teacher; every year she repeated the same lessons to a new group of children. She sees me.

"Manfred."

She has a few small wrinkles around her eyes, and a few extra pounds. I love this woman.

"I'm going to the town meeting. Do you need me?"

"No. Isn't it true that it snows less and less?" She turns toward the group at the table. "We have to put snow machines on all the runs; there's less snow, so we have to make it ourselves. It's expensive, but what can you do?"

Another conversation begins, this time about global warming. I walk away. It's been fifteen, twenty years since the glacier started to melt, and now they notice, because the tourists can't ski as they would like. I go to the meeting at the town hall. I listen but don't talk; Albert is there, and he is much better informed than I am. After all, I was only a guide, I used to walk on that glacier as a kid.

I pick up my cane. At night my leg aches. As I get older it will get worse. I need to keep the other leg strong. I put on my jacket, the one Luna bought for me. I don't talk, and I don't buy. Maybe it's the same disease?

It has snowed suddenly, out of season; during the Christmas holidays we had nothing. The town is all white like when we were kids, when we came down for Christmas mass. People would stare. And whisper, "Those are the Sane kids."

We looked straight ahead at the priest. We didn't need them. And here we are, going to the town meeting.

The Sane boys have wives, kids, hotels.

Even Stefan found a wife, a Slav, good-looking. They have a son. He thought he was so clever, but now he has a wife who bosses him around. She doesn't shop for him, or cook. She has him wrapped around her little finger. Go figure. Stefan is like a child who wants his sweets. We ask him why, and he always says the same thing: "She's the only one I can't lead by the nose."

Perhaps. But the truth is that she does as she pleases and he is at her beck and call. There's ice on the road; tomorrow we'll have to break it up again. I've gone from mountain guide to car parker, very impressive. The town is quiet. Clara is right to want to leave; when you're young you can do anything, you're stronger than any obstacle. You can run up the mountain without breaking a sweat; now I look at it through the window before falling asleep, like when I was a kid and I used to stare up at the Gigante. But back then you felt like a giant.

WHEN BIANCA PICKED up the phone I had to explain who I was.

"Marina, of course. How many years has it been?"

"Fifteen."

"We've changed everything up here at the lodge. It's all different now, except for the mountains, of course. They haven't changed." She laughs. "How is your baby boy?"

"He's big now, and I have a daughter as well. And yours?"

"Silvia is here. Gabriel and Christian are down in town. They're ski instructors now. Come up and see us, we'd love to have you."

Children are running in the sitting room of the hotel. Mothers talk, and I can hear snippets of their conversations. "I don't want to put him to bed too early, or he'll wake me at the crack of dawn."

This is my first trip on my own. I've imagined it for a long time. Mario was surprised.

"ALONE? ARE YOU sure?"

"You have work, and the kids have school. Just for a week."

"Why do you want to go there? You never wanted to before."

I am not afraid he'll understand; he has no memory of that month. There are no photos in the album.

"I was alone. It was difficult. Marco never slept, and he hurt himself. I didn't think I was going to make it."

He stares at me, but he knows I have trouble expressing myself. "So then why do you want to go there?"

"For that reason. Because it was hard."

He smiles. "You want to return to your old battleground."

HE HAS NO idea how close he is to the truth.

I go to bed at ten. In the elevator I pass a father holding a bottle of milk; he's going to warm it up in the kitchen. I open the door to my room and turn on the light. Standing there in that room with the neatly made bed, the little curtains, the darkness outside, it all comes back. It never went away. Where was it hiding all this time? I feel light-headed. On the bed, as I clutch my knees to my chin, I feel the pain, but I can't cry.

I'm here. Come to me.

I breathe in, stand up. Stop this. It's a fantasy I've been nurturing for fifteen years. Everybody has one, but it's time to stop.

I undress. I'm thin. After the second baby my breasts are smaller but still shapely. I rub lotion into my still-smooth skin. My face is thinner. He'll find me less attractive, but of course he'll be worse off, older. He already had wrinkles on his face; who knows, perhaps he can't even walk. Bianca will tell me.

I'm wearing a new, blue nightgown. I smooth my short hair behind my ears. My hair used to be long; the sink in the lodge was too small to wash it in.

Now they've renovated the rooms, and I look younger with short hair.

⌒

THEY'VE FIGURED OUT how to talk and talk without really saying anything. Let's just buy the snow machines and shut up. We all want them, so what is there to discuss? I'm leaving. After all, Albert is here. "I'm sick of this. I'm leaving."

"Are you coming up tonight?"

"Are you crazy? The hotel is full. Luna can't handle it by herself. I need to shovel snow and help the tourists dig out their cars."

He laughs. He has a mustache now, just like our father.

"You're crazy, Manfred."

"What? I'm just saying she needs my help."

I get up, trying to avoid being seen. He calls me back.

"Manfred?"

"Yes?"

"Did you see that the woman from the accident is here?"

"Who?"

"The woman who called the police the night you fell."

I'm frozen, still bent forward. "Are you serious?"

"She's staying in town and coming up to the lodge tomorrow. She called Bianca."

"No, I didn't know. Ciao."

"Ciao."

I leave the meeting room. In the hallway more people are discussing the snow machines. I zip up my jacket and walk to the piazza, away from home. My leg hurts. It's best not to stand still in the cold.

What should I think?

I remember when I was in the hospital, when Luna told me that her husband had come to pick her up.

I told her to leave.

And when I returned her letter to her.

You did the right thing, Manfred. You're not like that American; you would never take away someone else's wife.

In the letter she thanked me, but underneath she wrote: I kissed you, and I want to kiss you again. She would raise her fist at me again if I said it, because it's the truth.

Perhaps I shouldn't think about it at all, forget about it as I have all these years. Except that one time.

WE CONVERTED THE house into a hotel and launched it with a party. Half the town was there, and of course my brothers, father, and nieces and nephews. We were also celebrating the fact that I was walking again. The rehabilitation was long and hard, and I had a lot of help from Luna and the kids.

We ate and danced. Not me, of course, but I've never danced, even before, and now at least I had a good excuse. Stefan danced with Luna; he always had a thing for her, but then he likes every woman. I imagined her in Luna's place in Stefan's arms. I felt a surge of anger, for letting her go, for throwing her back into her husband's arms. I felt like a fool. Luna stopped dancing and came over; she was happy, and she kissed me. My previous thoughts disappeared, washed away by a wave of shame.

I dream about her at night. I'm buried in the snow. She kisses me, as she did at the hospital. I feel the heat of her mouth in mine, but I can't pull myself away. The Snow Queen; she warms you up and then leaves you.

SHE'S ON VACATION with her husband. Maybe the boy is here as well. How old is the boy? Seventeen, eighteen? A young man. They've come to spend a week in the mountains.

That's the way to think about it, Manfred.

2

THE LODGE IS covered in snow; I can't see the rocks. It looks different. I climb out of the snowcat. A young man drives. He says to me, "I've been working for them for a few years. There are a lot of visitors, and they can't manage on their own."

"And Silvia?"

I think I see him blush.

"She works with her mother."

We are surrounded by snow, loosened by the snowplows. The guide drives steadily up an unmarked path, through the blank, white landscape. I have only been down it once, at night, in summertime. Marco was in my arms, and there were other people too. This time I'm alone. I don't remember his face as he slept. Now, I take pictures of them so I won't forget their faces as children. But I have no pictures from that month. I remember how I held him in my arms, his eyes closed, his head

against my shoulder. His hair has grown over the spot where
they shaved his head, and the scar. I wonder what, if anything,
he remembers of that month.

A CONVERSATION WITH him at the table.

"You were always moving, and sometimes you would fall
and hurt yourself."

"It's your fault, Mamma, you didn't pay attention!"

I'm silent. What does he know? My silence worries him.

"Come on, Mamma, I'm kidding!"

"No, you're right. I was distracted. Your father used to scold
me. And you were always moving! Silvia was calmer."

"I tested your patience, didn't I?"

"Yes."

"That way you couldn't forget me."

He laughs. He sounds like Manfred. One time I mentioned
his name, to create a connection between them: "Our landlord
was a mountain guide. He drove us to the hospital. He found
me hiding behind a door, because I didn't have the strength to
look at you."

He listens and imagines his mother, all alone, unable to take
care of him.

"Good thing he was there."

"Yes, it's true."

THE YOUNG MAN follows me with my suitcase. We sink
into the snow. I push open the front door. Everything is new,

the wood paneling on the walls, the counter, everything but the stuffed woodchuck, standing on its hind legs, and the sled. There aren't many people in the foyer or the dining room; they're still out on the slopes. A dark-haired girl greets me.

"Hello."

"Hello, I've reserved a room."

"Yes, my mother told me."

"Are you Silvia?"

She nods.

"I'm sure you don't remember me."

She shakes her head. Curtly, she asks the young man to take up the suitcase. She used to do what her brothers told her, and now she runs the place. I hand her my suitcase, and she takes me up to the second floor.

"You've renovated."

"Two years ago."

The room smells like fresh wood. There's a private bath, and a comforter decorated with little flowers. The suitcase is already on the chair.

"Is your mother here?"

"She's in the kitchen."

"I'll come down later and say hello."

When she smiles, she looks like the patient little girl who used to play with Marco.

It's cold outside; I lie down on the bed and wrap myself in the comforter. I could rent skis, or put on a pair of snowshoes and go for a walk, or read downstairs in the sitting room until the skiers come home. I'll go to the kitchen and say hello to Bianca.

What if no one tells him I'm here? He might never find out. And what if he knows already but isn't interested in seeing me? Better. But you don't really think that, Marina. He might do it out of spite. Maybe he can't walk, or he's not well, or he doesn't want me to see him.

I go downstairs to see Bianca.

I DIDN'T SLEEP, and this morning I feel cold. The doctors should explain this to me: why does this damned leg still hurt, even though I can't move it? I shovel frozen snow, and scatter gravel. They always need their blasted cars; there are buses every fifteen minutes, and you can walk the length of the town in half an hour, but it makes no difference. After all, Manfred can dig out the car. I complained to Luna this morning while I was getting dressed, and she scowled at me.

"What do you care, as long as they keep coming?"

"I know: the mortgage!"

"You're in a bad mood today, Manfred."

"As usual."

What is she doing here? If she thinks I want to meet her family, she's sorely mistaken. She went up to the lodge on purpose; she's probably been planning this for years, to show off her family. Or maybe to her this is just a place like any other. Manfred, you're a fool.

And what if I stuck a nail, just one little bitty nail, under the tire of this SUV?

～

WE USED TO do it to the jeeps that came up to the lodge when we were kids. Then we would laugh as we saw the faces of the tourists when they tried to drive away. We'd help them change the tire, and they would say to our father, "What good kids you have."

Our father was proud of us; he had no idea how happy we would have been if he had closed the lodge for good. I would have spent my days hiking in the mountains, and Albert and Stefan could have gone down to the valley to live the life they wanted. At Clara's age, we did everything we could to get out of here. Thinking about my mother, I could almost sympathize with her decision. My father didn't know, nor did he ask; for him, every day was the same. When I turned eighteen, my brothers and I talked through the night. Even I, normally so reticent, asked questions: "Will we end up like him? I'm not getting married, and I don't want a house, or kids."

Albert already had Bianca. "If we get married, I'll lock the door every night."

Stefan was still clueless. "I'll have three wives, that way if one goes away, I'll have two left."

LOOK HOW WE ended up. I finish shoveling the snow and head over to Stefan's. Maybe he knows why Marina came back here.

BIANCA PUTS THE kettle on. We're alone in the kitchen.

"Sit down. Would you like a cup of tea?"

"The table is the same, isn't it?"

"Yes, the table and the stove. The rest is new."

I sit down and touch the old wood. That day long ago, Marco ate here, with his hands.

"Soon the cook will arrive and begin to prepare dinner. I'll have to clear out. That's how they are; they don't want us underfoot. I used to do everything myself, but now I'm tired."

She has gained weight. In her face too. Her eyes are melancholy now. She has changed, like the kitchen. She turns around and faces me.

"You look well, even younger than fifteen years ago."

"I cut my hair. And in those days I never slept."

"So, you decided to take a vacation on your own. I should do the same. But who would look after Albert and the lodge? He doesn't want to go anywhere and Silvia and he don't get along. How is your son? You have two now."

"Marco is seventeen and Silvia is fourteen."

"Silvia, like my daughter."

"Yes, I gave her the same name. I've thought about those days I stayed here with you many times over the years."

She pours some tea. I warm my hands on my cup. She sits down.

"If it hadn't been for you, Manfred would have been in that crevasse all night."

I clutch the hot cup.

"How is he?"

"Very well. He can't use his left leg, but that's the only thing left over from the accident. They opened a hotel, and their kids are all grown up now."

The heat rises up from my hands to my face.

"Did they get back together?"

She laughs. "How could he manage without her? Then, when he was better, she got what she wanted. The life they had before didn't suit her, and she was right. And Manfred is different now."

I remember another kitchen, and my conversation with his wife. I remember how she said, "Who knows what will happen now, after the accident. Maybe he'll need me." She was right.

"I'm glad he's better."

"He's not as moody, and he's kinder, even to his children."

I drink my tea. From some dark recess, deep down, I feel a wave of rage rising. Why did I come here? Wasted dreams, fairy tales, secrets. The truth is simple: he went back to his wife and found peace.

"We can call them. He'll be happy to know that you're here."

"No, that's all right. I'll go by and see them when I return to town."

STEFAN STARES AT me. His hair has gone gray earlier than mine.

"I had customers. Couldn't we talk in the shop?"

"Your wife can help them."

"It's cold out here. You didn't give me time to grab my jacket."

"Let's walk, that way you won't feel it."

I never ask him for anything, and here he is, complaining about a little bit of cold. Cars, the smell of gas just like in town, and the dirty snow.

"She's back."

"Who?"

"The one who called the police when I fell."

He thinks for a moment. "Oh."

"After all this time. Why? She's up at the lodge."

"What do you care? Maybe she's on vacation."

"Yes, that occurred to me. Maybe she's here with her husband and son. Perfectly normal."

"Yes."

"So I don't need to go up to the lodge?"

He stares at me. He thinks I've gone mad. "What for?"

"To say hello. I owe her something, don't I?"

He's frozen stiff. His words run together. "When did you become so polite?"

Stefan gets on my nerves. "So it would be dumb to go up there?"

"No. In fact, she might be glad to see you."

"Thanks. Bye."

I leave him there in the street. Stefan has never understood anything. I won't go up to the lodge. If she wants to see me, she can come to me.

I EAT BY myself in the dining room and I don't know where to look. If I settle my gaze on one of the other tables, it's invasive; if I stare into space or up at the stuffed deer, I look crazy. Tomorrow night I'll bring a book. This morning I took a walk, but it was cold. I never liked skiing. I fell asleep under the comforter, and when I woke up it was light again.

I want to see him because I owe a debt to him. I pull the photos of the kids out of the envelope and call home, but no one is in. I'm all alone, as I was that month. There is a dark cloud inside of me, deep, deep down. For months and years I don't feel it, and then it comes to the surface. Whom can I tell? One night I had a fight with Mario, but it doesn't happen often; I know how to control myself.

HE WAS CALM. The angrier I got, the quieter and colder he became. The subject of the argument was something absurd; we were really arguing about something else, something unsaid. My rage is the reason for the fight. He can't see me this way; he can't accept it. I'm not the woman he married, years ago.

On that day, the baby stared at me with terror in his eyes, first in my arms, then on the floor. Who is this woman? Even now, Mario is afraid of going deep. I no longer fear it, not anymore. I hold his fear up to his face and laugh.

"This is me, Mario, this is who I am! There are men who aren't afraid of me!"

He stares at me in silence. "Have you known many?"

"One." I cover my tracks with a lie. "Before I knew you, when I was on a trip."

"You should have married him."

"He didn't want me."

He gets angry: jealousy, wounded pride. But now I know who Manfred is: the only man who is not afraid of me. I said it, just like that. I hold him close, separate from everything else.

~

ALBERT COMES OVER to my table to say hello.

"Did you go skiing?"

"No, I went for a walk. I'm not much of a skier."

"Last night I saw Manfred and I told him you were here."

I smile calmly. "I'd love to see him. Bianca told me that he's well."

"Yes, he's less of a bear than before. Sometimes Stefan and I miss the old Manfred."

"How is Stefan?"

"He's married with a kid. After dinner they'll come up; come have a drink with us."

He walks off. Stefan was a good dancer. He knows I'm here. Stefan comes up to the lodge but he doesn't. Why should he? Just wait, Marina, one day, two days. Let's see how long he stays away.

EVERY NIGHT IT'S the same thing. If I want to talk to Luna I have to wander among the tables, smile, say hello.

"Good skiing today, Manfred!"

"I'm glad to hear it."

"What's the forecast for tomorrow?"

Maybe I'll say it: storms, wind. No, I can't. We have to pay the mortgage. "No snow, but it'll be sunny."

He smiles. No matter what, he's happy.

Luna makes small talk. She never gets tired. She sees me and then turns toward the customers: "Please excuse me a moment."

She comes over and I ask her in a whisper: "Where is Simon?"

"He went into town to see his girlfriend."

I feel the anger rising and without realizing, I raise my voice. "He goes every night!"

Luna pulls me into the kitchen. "Why are you angry?"

"Who'll work behind the counter? Do I have to do it?"

She peers into my face. "Do you need to go somewhere?"

"Nowhere. I want to go to bed. Tomorrow I have to get up early to go up to the lodge."

"Go to bed. I'll handle it."

Her calm makes me crazy.

"He should be here."

She stares at me the way she used to, when she suspected me of something.

"He can only see her at night."

"Poor thing! I'm here all day long, digging cars out of the snow. Stefan asks me if I want to go up to the lodge, because he's finished for the day. But no, I can never go, because Simon is in love."

"But you said you want to go tomorrow early!"

She always gets to the point.

"I already told him I can't go tonight, but I'd like to go to bed."

I turn around and walk away. She's wondering why I'm angry, but it doesn't matter. She has patience, but I don't. There's a limit. I have a bad leg, I can't work as a guide, I'm married, with adult children; I didn't want a house, and now I have a hotel, and only one day off a week, like the cook.

When I climb up the stairs, I can't hide my leg. I'm glad I didn't go up to the lodge tonight. She's not the type to let something like that go.

"Poor man, he can't hike up the mountain anymore."

If only one of my own kin had said it, just once. Everything's fine; you're lucky to be alive. What do they care if I miss my work? What do they know about what eats at me?

When you're on the mountain, if you scream or don't say anything at all, no one asks you for an explanation. You put one boot in front of the other, your blood warms up, you sweat, and there's nothing between you and the sky. If it's stormy, even better; the rain lashes your face, and you struggle to advance with your head down. I'm not afraid of dying, but she dragged me out of that hole. I can't complain; I'm alive, I have a family, a hotel, my brothers.

I lie down on the bed, finally alone.

Stefan takes his car, loads up his Slavic wife, and drives to the gondola station. Then they go up to the lodge in the snow-cat. They spend an enjoyable evening with her, drinking, talking. Perhaps they even talk about me.

"He was lucky; if you hadn't called the police . . ."

You don't think about it for years. If she hadn't come, my life would have been all set. Parking cars, arguing with my kids, paying the mortgage, going to bed early. You can't say it, but it's the truth. That's why I don't talk. What's the use of getting upset? Be calm, Manfred, you didn't go, you didn't fall for it. That other time you were younger, and you weren't ready to settle down.

She made a fool of me, dancing with Stefan, striking up a friendship with Bianca. She kissed me on the bed when I couldn't move. I grabbed her hand to keep her there but then I told her to leave forever with her child. He must be grown up now; a long time has passed. It's better not to think. I'll go tomorrow.

STEFAN HAS GRAY hair; I wonder if Manfred has gone gray as well. Albert is thinner; perhaps he is too. Stefan's wife tells me about Belgrade. She orders her husband to pour her a drink, without looking at him. Stefan smiles; he's happy to see us talking. When he arrived, he embraced me and presented me to his wife.

"Marina, a tremendous dancer!"

I laughed. "Not as good you!"

She didn't laugh. She stared at us suspiciously. So, to smooth things over, I asked her about her country. She warmed up, told me about the war and about her arrival in Italy. If it weren't for the war, Stefan would never have met her, and perhaps he'd have a different wife.

Husbands and wives are interchangeable. No one says it, but that's what I believe. You meet a man, you like him, his voice, his body, how he eats, how he touches you, your kids, the house. You lie in bed and you don't know which leg belongs to whom; but you don't remember why you chose that particular man.

I'm tired of her war stories, but she keeps talking.

"I left Belgrade with my mother."

Stefan smiles: "And then she met me."

She turns toward him with a brazen look: "That's right! I met him."

Albert laughs. "You married the handsomest of the three of us, and the biggest rascal."

Bianca taps her brother-in-law on the back. "It's not true. He's a wonderful husband."

Stefan smiles, a smile that is aged by his gray hair. "I pay her to defend me from my wife."

Everyone laughs, except his Serbian wife.

"I'm the foreigner here, and the last to know all of you, and I'm telling you that the best of the three is Manfred."

I was about to get up, but I change my mind. The two brothers and Bianca tease her.

"You wouldn't have lasted an hour with Manfred."

But Stefan's wife isn't bowed. "I'm not joking. It's true. He's quiet, he has a nasty streak, but at your father's funeral he was the only one who spoke at the church."

I can't help myself, I have to ask; who cares if they find me overly interested: "What did he say?"

Albert wants to drop the subject, but Bianca intervenes: "I couldn't believe it myself. He hadn't told anyone he was going to do it. When the priest asked if anyone had something to say, he stood up and went to the altar. He said that Gustav was a shining example of how one keeps faith in a commitment; that he had raised the three of them without coddling them; that they were lucky to have had him for a father."

The two brothers are visibly uncomfortable. The memory is too intimate. After a short pause, Stefan's wife adds, "At the end, he said, 'You can judge a man by the strength he shows with the people he loves.' I'll never forget it."

Albert snickers. "Our Manfred is a tough one."

Stefan looks over at him. "He was the same as a kid. If I cried, he didn't care. I could scream my head off and he wouldn't even look at me. As soon as I stopped, he gave me a piece of chocolate."

They talk about Manfred, his difficult personality, his wife's patience after the accident. I don't listen; I imagine him at his father's funeral, or giving his little brother a piece of chocolate after he stops crying.

I stand up. "I'm sorry, I need to go to bed. I'm tired. It must be from the traveling, the altitude."

I thank everyone and embrace Stefan and his wife. Bianca walks upstairs with me and hands me the key and a bottle of water.

"Sleep well."

I TOSS AND turn in bed; I might as well have stayed downstairs to help Luna. I have to admit, the idea that she's here, nearby, makes me anxious.

After fifteen years, she was dead, like my leg. I never brought her back to life, out of fear that the mere idea of her would make the blood rush through my veins as it does now. The blood pulses in my head, in my hands, in my chest. It's best if she leaves immediately. Part of me thinks that, but another part wants to see her. I tease my son, but I'm no better than he is.

Fifteen years ago, she was a different person; maybe she has left her husband, has been with other men, it wouldn't surprise me. Maybe she doesn't even remember that you live here. Be realistic: 365 days by fifteen years since you last saw each other. First multiply by ten, then by five.

Five thousand four hundred seventy-five days. Well done, Manfred, you still know your multiplication tables. But you're still awake.

THE STRAP OF my nightgown slides down my shoulder. I bought it before coming here, along with a new set of black underwear and bra, all for an aging mountain man who has gone back to his wife.

Standing in front of the mirror, I touch my lips. It's typical of women, dreaming of something they can't have. He doesn't care about you, he has a life to live.

I stretch out on the bed. I came all the way here to see him; tomorrow I'll go down into town, I don't care what I find.

3

WIND, SNOW. THE customers are stuck in the hotel like mice, and finally I'm free. I walk and the leg doesn't bother me. I can't feel my chin or my cheeks. I reach the gondola station and come back. It's nothing, for someone who used to hike all the mountain passes around here in one day and knew every peak like the back of his hand. Now this is enough for me, especially today. There's not a soul around, no voices, just the dull sound of snow falling from the trees, the wind in my ears, icy needles on my sleeve.

"You want to go up to the lodge on a day like this, with your leg?"

"I'm just going to the gondola station and back. What do I care about the weather?"

She doesn't try to stop me. Luna knows me too well for that; and it's not like her to insist. This is how it has been between us since the accident.

⌒

IT'S NIGHTTIME. WE'RE home after two months in the hospital. Clara and Simon are sleeping. She has put her things back in the closets, and the house smells clean again. I get up twice a day to do my exercises; but I still haven't been able to walk around the whole house. I take my time. I don't want to see the pots and pans in the kitchen, the dishwasher on, their shoes in the entryway, her pantyhose and bras in the bathroom. She has decided to stay, but she hasn't told me yet. She's sitting on an armchair next to the bed while I pretend to sleep. She's been wanting to talk for days. I open my eyes. If it must happen, it's best for me to decide when. I ask her, "Aren't you going to sleep?"

She looks at me. She's tired, and there are dark circles under her eyes. She came to the hospital every day and took care of me like a mother—not my mother. She whispers, as if there were a dead man in the room.

"Manfred, the kids are happy to be back."

Women always talk about the kids first. I ask her, in the strongest voice I can muster, "What about you?"

She cries. I've pressed the button that releases the tears. It should affect me but I feel nothing, I'm not sure why.

In the first years of our marriage, we were on the same side. Then, after Clara was born, we were on opposite sides. And now?

"Do you think it will be better living with half a man than it was when I was whole, Luna?"

She shakes her head.

"So why do you want to come back?"

"You'll be able to walk again, Manfred."

She didn't answer me. That day or any other day since. I didn't press the issue, nor did she. Anything to avoid touching upon the real question: why did she come back?

She sits on the bed and puts her arms around me. I feel her next to me; a window bangs in the kitchen. The one who saved me from death has gone away.

FROM THAT MOMENT on, nothing touches me: my children's voices, those of my brothers, the sound of the wind, the snow. It's all a mere accompaniment. I must go back much further to remember a time when I felt something: the presence of the mountain, the pain inflicted by my mother, the hatred and pity I felt for my father and my brothers. It is as if that were all I ever had.

All because of this woman. She came and turned everything upside down. In another half hour I'll reach the gondola station and go up to the lodge. I'll see her, she'll introduce me to her husband, and we can put it all behind us.

THE GONDOLA SWAYS in the white light, amid a cloud of little white dots. It has already stopped twice. I'm alone with the young man who closed the doors. I asked him, "Is no one else coming?"

"Not many people come up in this weather."

I'm frightened when it stops and begins to bob up and down in the air. I grip the icy handrail and close my eyes. Why on earth did I decide to ride down the mountain in this storm? I want to go to him. I didn't sleep; his proximity and the comments about him from last night swirl around in my head, along with images from these last fifteen years and from my time here with Marco, the only time about which I remember every detail. They put wood paneling on the walls and covered up the little boy with the glasses and the wide-open mouth. Marco's wound, too, is concealed by his hair.

ONE DAY WHEN he was thirteen, after taking a shower, he came into the kitchen with a frightened look. His hair was combed back, his robe tied tightly, his white chest still slender and hairless. These were the last days of his boyhood. He said, worriedly, "I have a scar on my head, Mamma, look."

I didn't turn around. "Hadn't you ever noticed?"

"No. What is it from?"

"That time when we went to the mountains. You fell off a table, I told you about it."

"But it's a big scar. Did I have stitches?"

I turn toward him and smile, reassuringly. "One of the many hospitals we visited when you were little. You were impossible."

He touches the spot on his head: "A hidden scar. I like it."

I hug him and kiss him on the head. "Like a soldier."

He pulls away. "Come on, Mamma."

THE GONDOLA BRUSHES a pylon. I look up at the young man.

"Is it dangerous?"

He smiles. "No, don't worry. As soon as the wind calms down we'll start moving again."

Calm: the wind, my fury, and his. I was ready to leave everything behind, but he said, "You can't. Stay where you are."

I stayed, and so did he. His wife, his children, the hotel. Like dogs chained to a post. You try to jump, but you can't; you're chained, don't you remember? Is there anything else in life but this?

The gondola begins to move; we descend slowly in a cloud of white dots, rapping against the windows. I'll go to the house and ask for him; if his wife is there it doesn't matter, I'll just say, "I'm here on holiday, and I wanted to say hello."

All I need is a tiny sign, to understand whether it was all a dream, like the prayer I used to say before going to bed when I was a little girl: "Tomorrow at school, please, please, let him notice me."

If I look into his eyes, I'll know whether I'm still inside of him. Halfway down, the other gondola appears in the fog, traveling upward in the snow. Another box, just like mine, struggling to rise as I descend. One above, one below. Never in the same place, except at the moment of crossing. I think of him; I mustn't forget why I'm here. It's too easy to forget, to tell oneself that life is something else, that love and desire are just dreams.

I've always been the same, even as a little girl, just like my uncle, as my father used to say. The uncle who sang the song with my name. I've stopped following advice; forget the wise path, do what you want, suffer, discover things on your own.

Suddenly I see him in the other gondola, standing in the window. He's staring at me with his eyes and mouth open wide, like the boy in the drawing. "Manfred!" I yell.

The young man turns around. I don't care what he thinks, I need to know.

"It was Manfred, wasn't it? Where is he going?"

"He's going up to see his brother."

I think to myself: he's coming to see me, you fool.

After a moment he adds, "There's too much wind. After this run we're shutting down the gondola."

He was coming to see me. Now what? They're shutting down the gondola. He's up there, I'm down here. Separated again.

"MARINA!"

What a fool; she can't hear me. She saw me. We looked at each other. Her hair is short.

"Who was that, Uncle? The woman who saved you?"

I turn toward my nephew. Christian leans against the opposite wall in his red ski instructor's jacket. He has Bianca's face and Albert's light-colored eyes. We're alone with the lift operator.

"How do you know?"

"Silvia told me. She was up at the lodge."

I think to myself: why is she coming down?

"Is she here with her family?" I ask.

"No, I don't think so. She's on her own. She had a little boy; I remember him. They spent a few days with us."

She's here on her own, without her husband. Calm down, Manfred, she didn't come for you.

Christian stares at me. What a strange boy he is. He is Albert's firstborn. When he was little he didn't talk much and followed his father around everywhere. Nowadays, after he finishes work he goes straight up to the lodge. He doesn't have a girlfriend, or so his father seems to think. He says Christian reminds him of me.

"Where's your brother?"

"It's Saturday; he's out with his friends."

"And you?"

He turns toward the gondola operator with a worried look, but he isn't listening, he's looking out at the snow. The wind whistles loudly around us.

"Are you shutting down?" I ask.

He nods.

She's at the bottom and can't come back up. I'm at the top and can't get back down. I can't make it down on foot with my leg. I could ask Albert to take me down with the snowcat. Why did she go into town? Where is she headed? Be calm, Manfred, think.

"Do you mind not being able to drive, Uncle?"

"No. I only miss not being able to walk like I did before."

"Why don't you have a car custom-made?"

Kids have no imagination.

"I hate cars."

She came here on her own, traveled up to the lodge, and came back down just when I decided to visit. Maybe she was planning to return, but she doesn't know that the gondola will close. And now what? She'll take the bus into town and spend the night. We looked at each other, and she made a sign with her hand. She waved; what else could she do? She called out my name; I couldn't hear her voice, but I saw it. I need to go back down and find her; I can't stand it. Don't run after her, Manfred, remember your father. Gustav didn't run after his wife when she left him.

IT'S NIGHTTIME, TWO days before his death. We are alone; it's my turn to stay with him. I fall asleep on the chair next to the bed. When I wake up, he's staring at me. His once-strong voice is a whisper: "Manfred, go to sleep."

"I was sleeping."

"Go to bed."

"I'm fine. Why don't you sleep?"

He stares at me in silence, then says, "Things with your mother didn't go the way you think, Manfred."

I want to get up, but he gestures for me to sit. I must obey him, like when I was a boy. He's dying.

"She couldn't stop thinking about that man. She told me, in tears, and asked me to help her. She didn't want to leave us. I told her to get out, and that if she stayed, I wouldn't want her around anyway."

He pauses. He can barely speak, his breathing is labored. "Never run after a woman."

When he stops, I think to myself, You coward, she asked you to help her and you didn't keep her from going.

Then I'm ashamed for thinking it, and I say, "You were right."

He falls asleep. I look at my father, the man who took my mother from me.

I MUSTN'T GO down and look for her. She's alone and free. She left her husband, her son is grown up, and she's going around making trouble. She cut her hair. Why did she come here?

We've almost arrived. The gondola operator looks over at me.

"We're going to shut down for the day and drive back. Do you want a ride in the jeep? You can't walk down in this weather."

The wheels reach the track. Never run after a woman.

"No, I'm going up to the lodge with Christian."

WALKING TO THE café through the snow is hard going. In no time I'm covered in snow and my face is frozen. There are some skiers inside, drinking and warming up. But no one is out, just a few daredevils. Just him and me. I sit down. I know why he went up to the lodge. I can see his frightened eyes as they see me through the glass, silent words.

It's you, you've come back, it's been an eternity, where have you been, wait for me.

I sit down at a table. Fine, stare at me. I'm alone, I have no skis; I came here looking for a man.

"Would you like something to drink?"

The girl has an innocent face. I was like her once. I wore flowery dresses, an apron, and I pushed Marco around in his stroller, by myself. I passed the days, one after the other, without knowing where they were leading me.

I order a cappuccino; she cleans the table.

"How long until the bus leaves?"

"Half an hour."

How long should I wait? What if he doesn't come? What would Marco and Silvia think if they saw me? "That's not our mother sitting there waiting for a man."

And how about Mario? He has never known that I might leave him, that for me none of this was natural. That I still want to dance, to flee, to inflict pain. I'm not betraying them; I never made a promise to them. But I made a promise to him.

"Don't leave the boy."

The girl brings my cappuccino.

"How long does it take to get back down from the lodge?"

"The gondola is closed."

"What if someone wants to come down?"

"They'd have to take a snowcat or a jeep."

"How long would it take?"

In this weather, an hour.

I'll wait for him until the last bus.

THE HEADLIGHTS OF Albert's snowcat come closer, disappear around each bend, and reappear. We wait for him in the cold, uncle and nephew, at the corner of the broken-down wall of the gondola station. I hear my father's voice: "Battle on!"

HE USED TO pick us up here, after school. Stefan would fall asleep inside the bunker, even though it is open and just as cold inside as outside. But inside you feel the wind less. It was evening, and the gondola was closed, like today. I liked to imagine a running battle, shooting, dead bodies. The four of us fighting against the rest of the country, the school, and the outside world into which my mother had disappeared. In my mind's eye, we crouched by the embrasures, with our rifles and grenades at the ready, holding back the hordes that advanced toward us, the enemy. Stefan was a fallen soldier, and Albert and I guarded him. The general came down the mountain to save us. We would bury Stefan up at the lodge, with full military honors.

Fallen in defense of the Land of the Sanes against the invaders.

I used to dream of an enemy that never came; our mother and the American were far away.

MAYBE SHE WENT down to see friends in the valley. She'll take the bus into town.

Christian puts on his cap and claps his hands together for warmth. I tell him, "After school, your grandfather used to come and pick us up here."

He looks over at me. "Dad told me."

We all tell our children the same stories, as if trying to attach them to these rocks. Clara was right to leave.

"What are you going to do at the lodge on a Saturday?"

I want to provoke him. He shrugs.

"I want to relax. Every day I take the kids out to ski with their parents. I can't stand to hear them."

"Don't you have a girlfriend?"

He stares at me; he didn't expect this question from me. For several minutes he says nothing.

"She left me."

His parents don't know.

"A girl from the town?"

He pauses again, unsure of whether it is a good idea to discuss such matters with me. But he wants to talk.

"No. She used to bring her kid to me for lessons."

"Was she married?"

He nods. I don't know what to say.

"How old was she?"

He shrugs. "I don't know."

He hangs his head and leans against the wall with his eyes closed.

"Where did the two of you meet?"

He looks like he's about to cry. "I would wait at the bar, and she would call me when her son was asleep."

He would down his last drink, pay, and run to his rendez-vous. How he misses her! How I miss her. I feel a dull pain, like the one I felt back in the days of the wars of the Sanes against the world. Then the kiss on the hospital bed, the saliva. Leaning against the walls of our childhood, covered in snow like two soldiers, we dream of the warmth of bodies embracing after a long wait.

The beams of the snowcat come closer, cutting through the snow. I turn toward the gondola station. The jeep is still there.

~

THE WINDOWS OF the bar are misty; I rub a circle with my glove. The ski runs are deserted and the mountain is bathed in mist; the bus is about to leave for town, and then there will only be one more. Two more runs before the bar closes. The young girl with the innocent look told me. She took the cup and placed the coins in her apron pocket.

"Are you waiting for someone?"

"No." Then I change my mind. "Yes." I blush.

Will there be another bus tonight?

She glances over quickly. "One more, then there's only the jeep for the gondola operators, which takes us down."

I look at the three men at the bar; they drink and laugh with the other waitress. The girl looks over as well.

"They never leave until we throw them out; it's the same every Saturday."

The last bus, with three drunkards. Manfred has no intention of coming down. Why should he? He's probably with his brother.

I peer through the circle in the window. A few snow-covered skiers remove their skis and climb onto the bus. I should go with them; in half an hour I'll be in town. I'll go back to the hotel where I slept the first night. Tomorrow I can return to the lodge and pick up my suitcase. Just like last time, but in reverse: then, we left our clothes down in the town and we had nothing to change into.

That night I thought about him before falling asleep, filled with desire and the fear of being discovered. The next day he saw me standing in the window, my hair wrapped in a towel. Over the years, I had forgotten the details, but now they are coming back, one by one.

We drove down the mountain in the jeep as the baby slept. Manfred didn't come with us. His car never appeared. I peered out of the window and traced his path down the mountain, over and over. Up and down, and how long would it take, and where is he, and why hasn't he come? Like now. Finally, I called the police. I couldn't sleep; I can't sleep now.

We're on the same path, Manfred, you on one side, and me on the other. There's no reason for him to come down but one: he knows I'm here, he saw me.

The bus departs, passes me by, and disappears in the mist. The three drunks are singing now. A final prayer.

Manfred, come down; don't leave me here with them, don't leave me alone like you have all these years.

I SAY TO Christian: "I'm going to my woman. It's Saturday night; I want to be with her. Tell your father."

He nods. "Say hello to Simon."

He thinks I mean Luna; it's better that way. I'd like to say something to comfort him; his eyes are still moist. But there's no time. The snowcat comes closer. I don't want to meet Albert, and the gondola operator is walking toward the jeep with the technician. I try to run with my bad leg; the young Manfred runs next to me, his heavy boots, always a size too big, beating against the ice. My ears used to stick out under my hat, and my mother would blow on them to warm them. I stop next to the jeep, my hand on the door handle. I don't care who they are or where they're going, but I want a spot in the jeep.

"I'm coming with you."

They peer at me. "We have to load up the others, at the bar."

"Don't worry; I'll get out and take the bus."

As I sit in the backseat, images go through my mind. I press my hands together to keep from going mad. The two men in the front ask questions, talk. I close my eyes so they'll leave me alone. The technician says to the other one, "Poor Manfred."

They don't know that I'm going to meet my woman. She's different from the women around here; she dances, and she's small, brown-haired, with tiny breasts; she lies, gives herself airs, and cuts her hair. I have to catch her, stop her, press her to me until it hurts. That way she'll stay with me at school, in the classroom and in the schoolyard at recess. She's all mine, private property, don't touch. If she's not there, I'll kill myself. I should be dead, after all; I'm alive because of her, and now she's here and she doesn't want me. I'll kill her and then I'll kill myself, after all life is an endless bore, like these two talking and talking about nothing, about the snow, about the machinery, about money.

Wait for me, Marina. I won't let you go. First I'll undress you and stare at you, naked, in the little girls' room, before you pull up your panties and your stockings; I'll make you blush with shame. But in truth it's all you've ever wanted, ever since we started school. On the very first day you tripped me in the hall. You giggled with your friends, and I put a cricket in your notebook and you started to cry. Even if you run away, I'll find you.

The jeep hits something in the road. We fall back on our seats, and the motor stalls.

"What was that?"

The two men in front have gone quiet with fear. I get out, and my legs sink into snow up to my knees. The others follow. A tree lies across the road. My bad leg refuses to follow me; I fall, get up, pull my leg out of the snow with my hands, turn around, and scan the road. I scream in order to be heard.

"If we move it a couple of yards we can get by. Where are the ropes?"

The technician says nothing. He follows orders. I tell him where to tie the rope—not around the trunk, but the branches.

"We'll pull it by the hair, where we can get a better grip."

We pull, yell, and swear, but the tree barely moves and our feet slide against the ice and sink into the snow. If I had two legs I'd leave them here and walk down.

I would have liked to run down the mountain in the fog, like a snowman, with icicles in my eyebrows and white hair. She wouldn't have recognized me at first. I'd grab her and melt, leaving puddles on the floor. It's me, Manfred, can't you see me?

Instead, here I am, struggling with a car, as usual. My curse! Now I pull with all my might, as if I were hanging above a void, two thousand meters up; just one slip and you're dead. The rock face obstructs the rope; it doesn't move unless you pull at it with your whole body, every muscle, tendon, nerve, and thought. Once, when I was climbing the rock face, at the toughest point, I had an erection, as if I wanted to fuck the rock. Now, as I pull, I think of Marina, about how I know everything about her, with just one look, and at the same time I know nothing.

That's the beauty of it: you know everything and nothing about this woman you are running to.

DAMNED BUS; IT'S there, waiting for me. The drunks are already on board; I can hear them screaming and laughing. The driver tells them to be quiet, but after a moment they start again. They call out to me from the window: "Aren't you coming? You're the last one."

"I know, but I still have a few minutes."

The café is closed. The waitresses are waiting for the jeep. It's late. They just called; there's a tree blocking the road.

"Perhaps I could wait here with you."

They peer at me. "Hasn't your husband arrived yet?"

I shake my head.

"Do you want us to send word?"

"No, thank you, he must be up at the lodge."

They look at each other. "There's not enough space; there are already two men in the jeep, and we have bags to carry."

"Will there be other jeeps?"

"Not in this weather."

I go up the steps and into the bus. It reeks of wine. The floor is wet with melted snow; there are muddy footprints. The three men fall silent as I walk by, then I hear a whistle. I pass a couple of frozen skiers, sitting close together. I go to the back of the bus, as I used to on school trips; you could do whatever you liked there, no one paid attention. I turn around; the road behind us is empty. He's not coming, it's clear. The last bus, the last jeep. I sit down on the cold seat. I take off my hat, the snow melts on my gloves.

My sisters used to tease me.

"Stop daydreaming, Marina, come back to earth!"

I pat the snow on my wool cap until it melts in wet splotches. He's like all the others, what did you think? Only you would wait for fifteen years, be a mother, a wife, learn how to cook, take care of the house, and work, while carrying that man inside of you. You bring him out into the light when you can, in the bathtub, sitting in the sun, between two lines in a book. You imagine the end.

The bus departs. I should call home.

"I'm fine, and you?"

I won't come back here. I rest my head against the window and close my eyes. There's no light, just a young girl's fantasies.

A SCHOOL TRIP. You sit in the back. The boy you like is in the first row. You close your eyes. You don't want the real him; it's better to just imagine him sitting beside you. An imaginary kiss. Someone on the bus plays a tape of love songs. It could just as well be another boy; you don't want a relationship, a boyfriend, a house, friends. All you want is for him to sit next to you while the music plays. You rest your lips against the foggy pane leaving an impression of your lips, and then another one. You were here.

I HOLD MY jacket close and stretch out in a corner of the bus. Nothing has changed; I'm still alone with my fantasies.

I CAN'T STAND these people. There are five of us in the car, and a mountain of plastic bags. They laugh and tell each other the story of how they cleared the road.

One girl turns to me; her thigh touches mine. She's young. "You're strong, Manfred."

"You have no idea how strong I was when I had two legs."

She laughs. The others tease her. She likes me. I should go home with her, to make the most of what's left of the day. I was born to fall on my face. Nothing ever goes right. I consider the pros and the cons, the probabilities, but in the end it all goes up in smoke. Things have a way of going their own way. Look at Luna; she got what she wanted, the hotel, the lame husband, and her children. I should have known from the beginning that I was destined to lose, after the whore left with the American. But I never give up; I keep running, I pull the rope, freeze my good leg while the other one sinks into the snow. And all on my day off. Just lie in your bed of shit, Manfred, you're used to it, and anyway, you can't break free.

And the conversations in the jeep! The older woman describes her husband's ailments, and then everyone mentions a relative who suffers from the same condition, a cousin, father, mother, uncle, brother-in-law, friend, friend of a friend, or a cousin's cousin. Suddenly the car feels like a hospital ward. Why do people love it when other people feel sorry for them? What do I care if they know how I feel? It doesn't make me feel any better. I was sure I would find her at the bar. We moved the tree out of the way; I jumped into the jeep, and I yelled at them to drive quickly.

"Go faster or I won't make it on the bus!"

They try to reassure me: "If it's gone, we'll take you down; we can all squeeze in, don't worry."

Even if she had waited, she would have had to take the last bus. I push them and criticize their driving; if I had my leg, I'd show them! When we get to the bottom, the gondola station is empty, the bar is closed, and the two women are there waiting with the bags.

"Where's the bus?"

"It left."

I look around, as if she might be hiding there in the mist, behind the empty gondola station.

They load the bags and talk about the tree on the road.

We're all squeezed into the jeep; the garbage bags reek of beer, and the bus is gone. If only I knew whether she had been there. Finally I decide to ask, what the hell.

"Was there a woman at the bar, waiting for someone?"

One of the women nods. My hands and cheeks are burning; something in me jumps for joy. She adds, "She was waiting for her husband."

It wasn't her. It's like a roller coaster, first up and then down. I settle in next to the girl in the jeep; soon, I'll be home, I'll take a shower, and I'll go down and help Luna. I'll spread gravel between the cars to make the job of digging them out easier tomorrow. My family is right: I should thank God I'm alive. Even if sometimes it seems to me like living and dying are pretty much the same. The others talk, or sit quietly. The curves throw us against each other, there is laughter. The young woman says to the older one, "If she had come with us, we would have been pretty crowded."

"Who?"

"The woman who was waiting for her husband. She didn't want to leave. I asked her why she didn't want to call him. It was strange; maybe they'd had a fight."

The young woman laughs: "Or maybe he left with someone else."

I sit up. "What did she look like?"

"Small, with brown hair."

4

IT'S DARK OUT. I can't see inside the bus. I stand near the door but not too close; I don't want to frighten her. The three town drunks climb off, followed by a pair of skiers. Young people dressed for a Saturday night on the town climb on. I've known them all since they were born. She's not there. I hesitate, and the driver looks over: "Do you need to get on, Manfred? Are you going to the city to have some fun?"

I don't answer. Everyone knows I'm not a big talker.

The jeep passed the bus on the road. There are no other stops, so she must be on it. I get on, dragging my leg behind me, tired, sweaty, my hair and face wet, hands aching. The kids stare; what is Simon's father doing here? Even if Luna were sitting among them, I would still go to the back to look for her.

She's in the corner, in the last row; it's dark, I can barely see her face, and I don't know if she sees me. I draw closer, trying not to limp; maybe she doesn't know about my leg. She can't see me. She's sleeping, that's why she didn't get off. I sit down near her but not too near, that way if she wakes up she'll have time to react. If I woke up with her sitting next to me, I would have quite a shock.

The bus leaves with a heaving of old metal. She doesn't wake up. In the light of the streetlamps, her face emerges from the darkness. With her short hair, her head looks small. It rests against the glass pane, so I can see only half of her face. She's breathing with her mouth open; maybe she has a cold. Her hands are tucked into her armpits; she's cold. Her hat is on the floor. I pick it up: it's black, with a red flower on one side. Who would wear a hat like that? I hold it up to my nose; the fragrance of it makes my head spin. I fold it and put it on the empty seat between us.

She can't leave now, there's no way. I'm sitting next to her; I can touch her. How can she sleep with all that noise, the kids screaming, the driver's radio, the squeal of the breaks, the curves in the road? She has to wake up soon; she's moving, she stretches, she adjusts her position, and then she opens her eyes.

IT'S FREEZING HERE. Where am I? It's dark. I'm still on the bus. How long is the ride?

I turn around; there's someone sitting there. I didn't hear him arrive.

Hold your wallet close and don't fall asleep, that's what my father told me. But I never paid him any mind. This man has wrinkled hands; I won't look at him so he doesn't get any ideas.

There are kids screaming. When did they get on? With all the empty seats, why did this man have to sit here? I put a hand over my eyes and between the fingers I glance over at him. I sit up. It can't be him.

"Manfred."

He looks older. His face is thin. Back then, his pale, sad eyes were hard; they never looked at me. I feel short of breath.

"When did you get on?"

"Just now."

It's him; the same voice. Of course it's the same voice, it's his voice. I run a hand through my hair; if only I had a mirror.

"I fell asleep."

"I know."

"Where is the bus going?"

"Into the city."

"I wanted to get off near my hotel."

He's a mess; where did he come from? Did he run? Where was he, how did he come here? I don't say a thing. After a silence, he speaks, amid the yelling and laughter: "How is your son?"

"He's grown up. I have a daughter too now."

She has a daughter. You can't have her, Manfred.

"How are your children?"

"Clara moved to the city. Simon is here."

Where should I take her? To a hotel, like Simon and his girl?

"Manfred."

Now she'll tell me why she came back. Women always take the first step. If only those kids would stop yelling, and the driver would turn off the radio with that horrible mountain music, always the same. Do I smell, or is it the bus?

She takes my hand and squeezes it. You're a man, Manfred, try to pull yourself together. It's not the first time a woman has touched you. She lets go.

"I saw you in the gondola and I decided to wait for you."

"A tree fell across the road, and we were stuck."

What I'd like to say is this: we're on the same road now, Manfred. No trees will block our path. But my mouth is dry, my face is warm.

"Why did you come back?"

How can he ask? I won't give him the satisfaction. "A vacation."

"That's what I thought."

Enough—we can't go back to the beginning each time.

"I came back because I wanted to see you again."

"Oh."

Stefan will know where I can take her.

"Manfred, we could have dinner together in the city. Do you want to?"

"Are you hungry?"

I laugh. "No, but that way we can talk, if you want."

"Talk?"

He hasn't changed. One word and we're standing naked in front of each other.

HE'S SWEATY AND lean. His skin is not smooth, but his muscles are strong. I caress the thin leg that he can no longer feel, and open my mouth to his.

Embrace me, Manfred, take every part of my body. It belongs to you.

Tiny breasts, flat belly, black hair between her legs. Her nipples are hard; she wants me. She knows how to move, how to make a man want her. Where did she learn?

He stops my hands, pushes them aside, as if we were locked in a wrestling match. He stares at me and says, "Wait."

"All right."

This mother of two has a young girl's body. If she touches me, I'll lose control. I know her. Who knows how many men she's been with; she plays with you, takes control. Don't lose your head, don't let yourself go.

He grabs my wrists. He's hurting me. He stares at me; my body excites him, but he doesn't touch me. Why? I ask him.

"Are you scared, Manfred?"

He smiles and the wrinkles on his face deepen. "Never."

"Why won't you let me touch you?"

He holds my hands but he can't avoid my gaze. His penis is stiff between his legs. "You're in a rush. You're too experienced."

Suddenly I notice details of the room. I feel cold. "Why do you say that? What do you want from me, Manfred?"

"Nothing. You're the one who came here. I wasn't thinking about you. I had my life."

I let my hands go limp and sit on the bed, on the cold comforter. I put one foot on top of the other.

"I've thought about you all these years."

Don't believe her. How can you know she doesn't say that to everyone? She walks into the hotel without shame and looks at the woman who gives us the keys without lowering her eyes. She undresses as soon as we walk into the room and puts her arms around me. Take me, look at me. Back then, she danced with Stefan just to make me look at her; now she embraces me, caresses me, and pounces. I won't let her lead me by the nose and then leave me, laugh at me. It won't work with me, Marina.

He sits in the armchair across from the bed. He has a small penis, like a child. What happened? We went into the hotel; I was embarrassed, but I didn't show it. I don't want to disappoint him. I want him, I'm already wet. The woman stares at me as if I were a whore; I don't care. We walk upstairs, hand in hand, and I'm happy. I don't see the room, only him, and I undress. My body belongs to him. His hands are on my breasts, on my neck, his tongue in my mouth. I feel everything as long as he touches me with his eyes. Then he pushes me away and looks at me with contempt. Hatred, incomprehension, rancor. So this is why I brought him here.

I've had other women, and I know I shouldn't show her how much I want her. It's better if I don't care, that way I can watch her and control the game. Start things, and end them as I want to. This woman has made my head spin. She's small and thin, with tiny breasts. Not my type.

I need to get up and gather my clothes. I feel ashamed sitting naked in front of him. I lower my head, trembling, and stare at the fold of skin on my stomach, my belly button. I feel dead. There are paintings of mountains, meadows, cows, and alpine streams on the walls. I can't cry, can't give him the satisfaction. I'll get dressed. I'll leave. I look up at him.

"It's cold in here. The room is depressing."

"This was the only place Stefan knew."

Who is this crippled mountain man, sweaty and mean, sitting in front of me, looking at me with indifference?

"Does he bring his girlfriends here?"

"Perhaps, before he was married."

These three brothers get older, fuck, get married, have children. For them, women must stay in their place.

"You Sane brothers are good husbands."

Now she's making fun of me.

"Not really. As you can see, I'm here."

Bastard.

"So you often go to places like this one?"

"Not really. Maybe you do."

His hatred has brought me here. Why?

"It's the first time. Maybe your mother came here, all those years ago, with her American."

She lands a blow. Don't stand up, don't react. That's what she wants.

"No, it was another city."

"Why can't you forgive her, Manfred? Always the same story. When will you get over it? Your father is dead now."

"She's dead too; a tumor. The American is still alive."

I get up. I'm too cold. I want to leave and never see him again, erase him from my dreams.

She's leaving. Let her go. That's how it has to end. She's putting on her underwear, looking for her bra, her stockings, trousers, and sweater. She picks up her jacket and the black hat with the red flower. I feel like a piece of ice, like I did in the hospital bed. She turns toward me.

"I'm leaving, Manfred. I shouldn't have come."

She turns away. I feel a pain in my chest. Darkness before my eyes. I get up and yell, "You're not leaving here."

I pounce, tear the jacket out of her hands, remove her sweater. My mouth is on her breast, now our mouths come together; saliva on my body, on hers, my hand between her legs. Marina, you are my woman, my flesh.

Touch me, Manfred, before I die again, this thing that binds us together forever.

5

NOW I KNOW. The life we lead, the one we choose once we've decided to be reasonable, is worthless. There are a few good things, like spreading gravel in front of the cars at six in the morning, even though none of those idiots will know that the reason they can move their cars is that you did your job well. There's no one around, and you, the house, the sky, and the mountains exist in the same silence. Or when you see Simon talking on the phone with his girlfriend. He's tall and stupid, but give him time and he'll grow up to be like Albert, the best of us. You see Luna and Clara leave the hotel arm in arm; you have no idea what they're doing, what they're saying, but they look happy. You watch them from behind the counter, and wait for their return. You're in the right place at the right time. But you can't hide the truth. If your life had begun differently, you would be with her.

I put down the shovel and go into town to have my first coffee of the day. Another solitary pleasure. The soles of my shoes

break the ice, every morning, as I walk down the hill. I can
see the piazza, and now I'm passing the bus stop; I stop for a
moment and see her in the hotel room in the city. I penetrate
between her skinny legs and come as I've never come before. I
feel a pain in my chest and heat in my bones; the coffee seems
almost cold to me. I'm the only happy man in the village, but
nobody knows it.

I don't know how long the feeling will last: walking by the
bus station every morning, imagining myself in bed with her,
with those paintings of flowers on the walls. Lying on the bed,
we play games, imagine where we'll go, the paradise no one
ever told us existed. These are days in another man's calendar.
Who knew a woman could harpoon herself to your body? It's
been two years and thirteen days. I'm strong, our father prepared us for sacrifice. Life is hard, but nothing prepared me for
this. If he were alive, I'd tell him.

The complaints about our mother and the American were
nothing compared to this. He called her a whore, forgot her,
took her children, burned her belongings, and left no trace of
her. This is my woman, Gustav, not my wife or the mother of
my children. Every day I try not to desire her, but I can't help
myself. You never told us how hard it is not to have the woman
you desire. Nothing binds us together, but I yearn for her body
as insistently as I do for my lost leg.

One day I went back to the hotel room; I rented it for a few
hours. I wanted to remember. Maybe one day I will walk by the
bus stop without seeing her.

The paintings, the bed, the armchair, the comforter. I found
myself on the floor, behind the bathroom door; she was there

but she wasn't. I started to cry, and I thought: if anyone saw me, they'd put me in the nuthouse.

ONE DAY LEADS to another. She left me her hat, the one with the red flower. She gave it to Bianca at the lodge, with a note containing two words. I tore up the letter. Like the letter she sent me the first time she left: words that mean nothing. The two words on the note are words we never said to each other. Neither of us. The hat is up at the lodge; Bianca kept it. She told me.

"Maybe she'll come back for it, or you can take it to her."

Marina trusts Bianca, and so do I. One day in the kitchen, I ask her, "What did she say?"

THE MORNING AFTER the storm, she was sitting where you are now. She was pale, and I felt sorry for her. I made some coffee and asked her what happened, where she had spent the night. She told me: "Manfred saved my son and me, Bianca. Nobody knows that."

"But you pulled him out of the crevasse."

"I wanted to stay, but he sent me away. I wanted to tell my husband not to come. Last night, we went to a hotel room in the city."

Her lips trembled, she grasped the cup in her hands. Later, she came down with her suitcase.

"I'm leaving today, Bianca. If Manfred wants me, he can come and get me this time."

~

I WALK INTO the bar. The man at the counter doesn't say hello. He hands me a cup of coffee. For a while now, I've been in the mood to talk, just to egg people on.

"I thought you had mellowed with age, Manfred."

Poor Luna. All she wants is peace and quiet. I provoke him: "Your coffee tastes like water."

He glances over. "So why do you come here every morning?"

"There's nowhere else to go."

He cleans the coffee machine, the bar, the sugar bowl. Around here, people clean everything as if they were possessed. Soap, disinfectant. Nothing tastes like anything.

"Wouldn't you like to know how to make good coffee?"

"No."

I stir it, hoping that the sugar at the bottom will give it some taste. I say, "A little dirt, the acrid tang of fried food, and a nice strong coffee. Just imagine what life could be!"

He goes on cleaning the machine.

"You know, it doesn't spout shit, only steam."

He turns around, red in the face, with angry eyes. He looks almost handsome; I'd like to take a picture and give it to his wife.

"Have you ever thought of going away, Manfred, and leaving us alone?"

I HELP HER with her leotard as she pulls tights over her skinny legs. I twist her hair and try to smooth it down with bobby pins, but the net keeps slipping through my fingers. Her hair is long, and I'm rushing, anxious.

"Mamma!"

"There's time. They haven't called you yet."

There are lots of mothers and daughters around us. Her hair must stay in place when she jumps. I see the other mothers' hands, fumbling like mine.

"Would you lend me some hairspray?"

We nurture their bodies, their spirits. They're strong, soft, light. They dance without boys, a kind of rehearsal. A mother near me says to her daughter, "Don't think too much. Just treat it like a lesson. Don't look at the audience."

I turn Silvia around and try to plaster down her rebellious curls. She stares at me with her dark eyes; she's scared. I bend down and whisper a secret into her ear; no one else must hear it: "Dance for him."

She laughs—she understands. She jumps in order to reach him, and thinks of nothing else. The boy sitting in the third row will never know, but it doesn't matter.

I kiss her. She runs off with the others. The mothers leave the dressing room, pushing to get a seat. I sit on a bench. There are girls' clothes everywhere: shoes, stockings, purses. All the preparations and expectations lead to this one moment that you will never forget.

I walk toward my seat and I feel him near me. It's always like that, a sudden pang, but it happens less often now. Sometimes a week will go by, once a whole month. I feel like I am walking toward him, not to the office or back home, but to the station to take a train. I bring my darkness and my icy cold; he can see them. He is the only one I haven't lied to.

The cold of the hotel room. One night together. We alone are warm; we never let go, even for an instant. What I'm doing here is also for you, even if you don't know it. Even if you've forgotten, even if you never come for me, if it was all a fantasy.

In the darkened theater, I go to my seat next to Mario. I'll stay there as long as I can. But even if I die without seeing you again, Manfred, I won't go to you; you must come to me.

The girls take their places onstage, trembling, arms extended. Mine is in the middle, waiting for the music to begin.

Do you really not feel me standing here, with my arms open wide? I've been waiting two years and thirteen days.

I LEAVE THE bar without answering.

Bastard, if he only knew how often I've dreamed of going away and leaving everyone alone.

I walk past the cemetery where my father is buried. The rage doesn't melt, like the snow on the tombstones. I imagine them together, my mother and my father, now that they're both dead and buried, one here, the other in America. I see them in front of the lodge, butting horns like two goats. It would have been better to have it out when they were alive.

I can't imagine staying here until the day they lay me down next to him. But if I go to her, what will I find?

CRISTINA COMENCINI is an Italian novelist, screenwriter, and director. Her 2006 film, *The Beast in the Heart*, based on her novel *La bestia nel cuore*, was nominated for an Academy Award for Best Foreign Language Film. *When the Night* is her English-language debut.

MARINA HARSS studied comparative literature and translation at Harvard and New York University. Her translations include Pier Paolo Pasolini's *Stories from the City of God* (Other Press), and *Conjugal Love* and *Two Friends*, both by Alberto Moravia.